Praise for Debbie Johnson

'A sheer deligh[t]'
Sunday Expres[s]

'Has all the best ingredients for a holiday read: the beautiful
West Country, a family-run farm, and a mystery man with
Poldark-style charms'
Yours Magazine

'The perfect summer story – a funny and moving read set in
glorious modern-day Poldark country'
Bestselling author Jane Costello

'A summer romance with an abundance of country charm,
Pippa's Cornish Dream by Debbie Johnson is a standout title
for this season'
Book Chick City

'A beautifully addictive read'
Reviewed the Book

'Just wonderful'
Lisa Talks About

About the Author

Debbie Johnson lives in Liverpool, where she spends her time writing, looking after a small tribe of children and animals, and not doing the housework. Her previous novels have included bestselling e-books *Cold Feet at Christmas* and *Pippa's Cornish Dream*. She also writes fantasy and crime fiction, to keep her out of trouble.

www.debbiejohnsonauthor.com

@debbiemjohnson

NEVER Kiss a Man in a Christmas JUMPER

Debbie Johnson

Harper
impulse
we've got the love

Harper*Impulse* an imprint of
HarperCollins*Publishers* Ltd
1 London Bridge Street
London SE1 9GF

www.harpercollins.co.uk

A Paperback Original 2015

First published in Great Britain in ebook format by Harper*Impulse* 2015

Cover images © Shutterstock.com

Debbie Johnson asserts the moral right
to be identified as the author of this work

A catalogue record for this book is
available from the British Library

ISBN: 9780008150235

This novel is entirely a work of fiction.
The names, characters and incidents portrayed in it are
the work of the author's imagination. Any resemblance to
actual persons, living or dead, events or localities is
entirely coincidental.

Set in Minion by Born Group using Atomik ePublisher from Easypress

Printed and bound in Great Britain

Chapter 1

The third time she encountered the man she now knew as Marco Cavelli, Maggie gave him a Christmas present to remember. A broken leg and two fractured ribs. Gift wrapped with a few facial abrasions and a very festive black eye.

Of course, it was all his fault. He was cycling on the wrong side of the road, in heavy snow, listening to loud music that drowned out her warning cries as the two of them veered towards each other. Two unstoppable forces, both covered in fluffy white stuff, both bundled up in hats, gloves and scarves. Only one of them looking where they were going.

Sadly, he took the ear buds out just in time to hear her cries of 'you complete arsehole', 'what the hell do you think you were doing?' and 'oh shit...hold on, I'm just calling an ambulance.' Ever the lady, she thought, adding a few even worse words in her own mind.

As she crawled across the ice to reach him, her jean-clad knees soaked through with icy snow, teeth chattering and fingers trembling as she dug her phone from her pocket, she decided that Sod's Law had well and truly shafted them.

It was her first day off in over a month. The first day she'd had entirely free from sequins and bows and velveteen loops and concealed zips and hooks and eyes and taffeta and lace. The first entire day free of pin-pricked fingers and nervous brides and half-cut mother-in-laws and last minute nervous breakdowns.

And what a day it had promised to be. Gloriously cold and frosty, the sky stretching overhead, a clear shining plain of dazzling blue; virgin snow turning the garden and the streets around her house into a joyful white confection.

Oxford in the snow. It was stunning, and never failed to knock her socks off. Though not literally, as she was wearing two pairs. She cycled carefully into town to do her shopping, excited beyond belief about what was waiting for her at the antiquarian book shop off the Broad. She'd been paying for it for months, and now, finally, it was hers. Briefly. Then, within a matter of weeks, it would be Ellen's. She couldn't wait, and realised as she pedalled up towards St Giles that there'd been a sneaky role reversal in her house: Ellen was too cool for Christmas now. It was Maggie who was the little girl.

Aah, who gives a stuff, she thought, as she navigated the slippery roads, keeping a careful look out for the bumbling backpacked tourists who wandered in front of her like blind sheep, and the few students who were still around.

Term had finished the day before, and the whole city had been clogged with cars – all loaded up to the rafters with duvets, dirty clothes and crumb-shedding toasters as they headed off home for Christmas. It was a different Oxford once they'd gone – quieter, less congested, but a lot less lively as well. They'd avoided the snow, which had snuck in like a thief in the night, laying an inch thick on all but the busiest roads.

She'd arrived safely, if a little soggy, at Kavanagh's Books of Note. She'd gleefully accepted the brown-paper wrapped package that had cost so much, and stashed it in her backpack before getting back in the saddle and heading towards the Covered Market, where she planned to treat herself to some hot chocolate and a small shed-load of tiffin. It was Christmas, after all. Almost.

Along the Broad she went, past the colleges of Balliol and Trinity, before veering off onto the ancient cobbles of Radcliffe Square. As she jiggled along, threading her way around the scarf-wearing academics heading to the majestic Bodleian Library, she noticed the lights were still on – it was after nine, but the hallowed halls of learning were still glittering with electricity, throwing tiny neon clouds through the glass. Must be all that dark wood panelling, cocooning them from the dazzling sunshine of the day. The steps up to it were dusted with snow, the cobbles coated and damp.

She was heading down the side of St Mary the Virgin, with its towering spire and dizzying staircase, looking all the more like a postcard through the fuzzy haze of still falling snowflakes. Inside, she could hear the sound of angelic voices rehearsing their Christmas carols – a crowd of undoubtedly less-than-angelic little boys transforming the Holly and the Ivy into something splendid and magical.

Then it was on, towards the High Street, accompanied by the random thought that Ellen might not like the book at all. That maybe she should have jacked in the idea completely, and given her the equivalent in cash. Maybe she'd prefer beer tokens to a first edition. Maybe she was just holding on to an image of her little girl that was long gone, eaten alive by the coltish young woman she now shared a home with. When Ellen bothered to come home at all, that was.

Later, she admitted to herself that possibly – just possibly – she'd been a little bit distracted. The much-used passage down to the High was relatively clear of snow, and she'd stepped up her speed just a tiny bit. Teeny tiny – so much so that her legs had hardly noticed the difference.

Sadly, that teeny tiny acceleration meant that when she saw the other bike – heading straight towards her and at what seemed like an impossible speed for a non-motorised vehicle to achieve – it was too late to do anything but screech like a banshee and hope for the best. Which was kind of her motto for life – she should probably get it printed up onto a T-shirt.

Catching a glimpse of startled, deep hazel eyes and a look of horror as he realised what was about to happen, they both attempted to swerve. Too late.

The next thing Maggie knew she was flying through the air, her bike free-wheeling into the wrought iron railings, the spokes crumpling and crunching as they slammed into them. She clenched her eyes shut as the world turned upside down, and braced herself for a crash landing. It came, with a dull thud, her backside skidding along in a pool of frost and slush and her helmet bouncing off the floor in a way that made her go temporarily cross-eyed.

For a moment she was too stunned to move. She lay there, feeling the moisture creep through the many layers of her clothing, a slow, paralysing sog of freezing cold snow wrapping itself around all her limbs. If this was a cartoon, she thought, Tweety Bird would be flapping round my head right about now. Wearing ear-muffs.

She lay still for a few seconds, allowing the fog to clear, before blinking her eyes and cautiously running a mental and physical check on her battered body parts.

Legs: yep, still moving. Arms: definitely all right. Head? A bit jiggered around, but essentially okay. Probably no worse than usual, anyway. It was only a searing pain running from her coccyx that was giving her any trouble. She'd landed on her arse – which, thankfully, had enough padding on it to have saved her from anything more serious. Three cheers for fat-bottomed girls.

She looked up and around, saw other people making their way towards them. Saw the man – the stupid, stupid man, with the big hazel eyes and the inhuman ability to cycle at 700 miles per hour – lying spreadeagled a few feet away from her, his few tortured,

4

jerky movements making an abstract art snow angel around his big, twisted body.

She crawled up onto her hands and knees, and inched in his direction, all the while yelling words of both anger and concern. He'd knocked her off her bike. He was an idiot, and deserved a good shouting at.

Her backpack had spilled open, and her precious edition of Alice in Wonderland was lying tattered and torn and dirty, soaking slush up into its beautiful illustrated pages. And her bum hurt. A lot. She felt like karate chopping him in the nether regions. Except... he seemed to be in a lot of pain. And that leg of his was kind of pointing the wrong way. And...shit, where was the phone? And why couldn't she feel her fingers?

As she got close enough to see his face, she realised who he was. It was Him. The Hot Papa from the Park. The Man with the Tux. The Guy Who Made Christmas Jumpers Sexy. The gorgeous American hunk-a-rama who had accidentally tripped in and out of her life over the last few days.

She glanced around, saw his bike. The bike with the child seat fitted on the back. The bike that was crumpled and buckled and lying abandoned by the rear wall of Brasenose College.

"The baby!" she shouted in complete panic as she finally reached him. "Where's the baby?"

Chapter 2

The first time she'd seen him had been less dramatic, but in its own way just as memorable. She'd been with Ellen, in the park. Three days earlier.

"I think I might die of oestrogen poisoning if this carries on," Ellen had said, looking on in disgust at the scene playing out in front of her.

"It's like all these yummy mummies have died and gone to totty heaven. Not a single one of them is watching their kids – they could be smoking crack or eating dog poo for all they'd notice. They're obviously all just thinking about shagging, and I now feel like I need to scrub my entire brain with bleach. I mean – come on, he's wearing a Christmas jumper! Surely it's in the feminist rule book that you should never kiss a man in a Christmas jumper? "

It was the first day of December, and the temperatures had plummeted overnight, as though the weather gods had consulted a calendar and decided to up their game. Ellen's invective was accompanied by a cloud of warm air gusting in front of her; and trainer clad feet kicked impatiently at the frost-rutted soil beneath the bench.

Her usually pretty face was twisted in contempt as she ranted, and she shook her head sadly as she unscrewed her water bottle.

They'd just reached the end of a three-mile run around the park, and Ellen looked untouched by the effort apart from a slight flush to her cheeks, and a few auburn tendrils clinging to damp skin.

That, thought Maggie O'Donnell, was what happened when you were 18, and your body hadn't yet been battered by life, childbirth, or too many nights in alone with Colin Farrell movies and a box of cream horns.

She herself had been battered aplenty by all three of those things, though at 34 she was still in pretty decent nick. Internally, at least. Not decent enough to have spare breath right at that moment, though. Instead, she attempted to smile at her irritatingly athletic daughter, sprawled on the bench next to her, and looked on at the playground panorama that had annoyed Ellen all the way into an anti-Vagina Monologue.

Maggie had to admit she was kind of right, even if she was being overly judgey. There was a man. A real life, honest-to-goodness man, invading the territory that usually belonged solely to the female of the species – at least on a week-day.

He wasn't just any old man either. He wasn't one of the harried stay-at-home dads who sometimes turned up, covered in pureed peas and scuttling from the nappy bag to the swings with as much joie de vivre as a hippo with a hernia.

No, this man was...well, frankly gorgeous. Tall – over the six foot mark anyway. Broad. Brawny. Dressed in cold-weather duds of Levis, a sweater – one with a giant snowman's face on it – and an expensive looking navy blue gilet. Dark hair that was starting to curl and looked like it was usually kept shorter. Yep – she could definitely see why the other mums had started to melt into a collective puddle of hormones on the frost-tinged grass. He looked like he'd stepped out of a rom com about a talented yet tortured rugby player.

She took a long drink of her water, sucked in a restorative breath, and continued to eyeball him as subtly as she could. Not, it seemed, quite subtly enough.

"Mum!" Ellen exclaimed, turning her piercing green gaze towards her. "You're doing it too! It's revolting – get a grip of yourself, you're behaving like you've never seen a man before!"

"Well, sweetheart, I'm not sure I've seen one quite like that for...well, ever. And you've obviously never watched *Bridget Jones's Diary* – a man in a Christmas jumper can be a force for good in the world."

Ellen snorted, staring at the sweater – and the man wearing it – in a highly unconvinced fashion.

"Anyway," Maggie continued. "Give a girl a break. I'm only flesh and blood, you know. It's not like you hit 30 and you stop noticing, as you'll discover yourself some day. And he is...easy on the eye."

As she said it, one of the besotted mums walked straight into the slide, she'd been staring so hard, clonking her head in pure Carry On style and blushing furiously. Maggie bit her lip to stop herself laughing out loud. There but for the grace of God go I, she thought.

"Stop staring!" said Ellen, not quite managing to keep the giggle out of her voice. "You're not a girl...you're an ancient old hag. You're well past your sell-by date."

"I am so *not*," replied Maggie, tearing her eyes away from the sexy stranger. "I may possibly be slightly past my best before date, but that's as far as I'll concede."

"What's the bloody difference, Queen of Tesco?"

"Well, if you eat something that's past it's sell by date, it's bad. Pretty bad. Like, potential food poisoning bad. Think granddad after that barbecue when he used up all the old chicken and took the radio into the loo for two days solid. But the best before date...

8

well, that's more of a guideline. Advice. If you eat something after that, it just means it's not at its best. It might not taste as good, but it probably won't make you throw up."

"And that's you, is it?"

"Yes, that's me. If someone – that man over there for example – was to eat me, I wouldn't make him ill, but he might have tasted better."

Ellen screwed her face up and made vomiting gestures with her fingers.

"I think *I* might throw up now...don't you realise it's your duty as my mother to remain a completely asexual being for the rest of your life? I like to believe that you've only ever had sex once – a majestic coupling that resulted in my entry into the world. I'm not ready to acknowledge anything more than that without trauma counselling. So stop leching and let's head home. I think you need a cold shower. Invite the rest of the penis-starved hordes to come if you like."

"Okay," said Maggie, laughing inside at the thought of the 'majestic coupling' that resulted in her getting pregnant at 16. Not the description most people would have used, taking place as it did in the back of a Datsun Sunny parked in a layby off the A40. "Message received and understood, Captain Puritanical. Just let me have five more minutes of acting like an asexual being perving over a complete stranger, and we'll be off."

Ellen harrumphed, crossed her Bambi legs, and stuck her ear buds back in to listen to music. Presumably to drown out the sound of the sighs whispering all around her.

Maggie gave her a sideways glance, then looked again at the playground. Apart from the man, the whole scene made her feel a little bit sad. Melancholy. The park was only ten minutes from their home in Jericho, and you could see the dreaming spires of Oxford city centre rising hazily out of the fog, distant and fuzzy and lit up like a Christmas tree made of mellow yellow stone. It was a beautiful view, and one that seemed to never change.

This was the park she'd been coming to for so many years now. There were distant, almost sepia-tinged memories of her own mother bringing her here as a kid. Then as a teenager herself – reckless and wild, swigging from huge plastic bottles of cider and spinning on the roundabout. A habit that may or may not have been related to the later majestic coupling in the back of the Datsun Sunny.

Then as a parent with a cute baby girl of her own in the pram, filling in the endless hours of life as a stupidly young mum, feeding the ducks and wondering what her friends were up to. And with Ellen as a toddler, Ellen as a little girl – and now Ellen as an almost-adult. If she closed her eyes, she could almost replay it, like a fractured dream sequence in a movie.

The swings might have had a lick of paint and the benches were new, but for Maggie, there were ghosts of Christmas past everywhere here, wrapped around the branches of every frost-tinged tree and echoing in every excited childish squeal she heard.

Ellen's childhood – those days you take for granted, where you're the centre of their lives – seemed a million years ago. The mums out there now looked tired, and messy, and frazzled like all mums do. They hadn't yet realised how precious these times were – and how fast you lost them.

She dragged her mind away from pointless, bittersweet memories, and back to the present. He was still there. The Man. Mr Tall, Dark and Handsome. It wasn't just the way he looked that was getting the ladies in a tiz – it was the way he was behaving with the little boy. His son, presumably.

A chubby faced cherub with unruly, deep brown curls, he was clearly what was known in the trade as 'a bit of a handful'. That – in school gate speak – could mean anything from a normal energetic tot to a demonically possessed alien being whose head could rotate 360 degrees while humming the theme song from *In The Night Garden*.

He was about two, and at that stage where they only have three settings – running, falling over, or sleeping. The Man didn't look tired though. He didn't look frazzled. Not a smudge of pea puree in sight. He was glowing with health and vitality, and keeping pace with the kid as he jogged from swings to slide to climbing frame, laughing all the time.

The Man was always there with a supportive hand, ready to catch the boy when he fell, ready to wipe mud of the knees of his jeans, ready to pick him up and swing him round in circles until the giggling had infected everyone within hearing distance. The Man sounded like he had an American accent, and he was calling the child Luca, which only added to the unexpected glamour of finding him here, on a grey, frosty day in Oxford at the start of December.

If he was aware of the fact that every woman in the playground was hoping he'd need a spare baby wipe or directions to the toilets, he didn't show it. He was focused on one thing only – being super fun time dad.

Yeah, thought Maggie, standing up from the bench and starting to stretch out muscles that were already sore. Asexual. Past my sell by date. And late for work.

Time to stop the drooling, and get ready for the rest of the day.

Chapter 3

The second time she saw him, she had her head up Gaynor Cuddy's skirt. Gaynor was the first of her Christmas brides, and had come in for her final fitting. She was a larger-than-life girl, Gaynor, and had ordered an even larger dress – in fact, Maggie had decided, it was entirely suitable to feature in an episode of Big Fat Gypsy Wedding. Even if Gaynor wasn't, to her knowledge, a gypsy, and instead worked as a call centre manager and lived in quite a swish flat off the Woodstock Road with her boyfriend Tony.

Hooped and embroidered to within an inch of its life, the frock was pretty much done. It had taken over a year to make, and about three miles of satin and tulle to construct. She'd exhausted the stock of every faux pearl merchant within a 100 mile radius, and risked permanent curvature of the spine, hunched over attaching them.

Now, after much trial and tribulation and detailed accounts of how little Gaynor had had to eat for the last month, it was perfect. Or, more accurately, it was perfect for Gaynor. Some of her other clients would faint with shock, but Gaynor was happy – and that was all that mattered to Maggie.

The reason she head her head up the skirt was to fiddle with the bridal under-garments. In keeping with the OTT frock, Gaynor had decided she wanted to have a garter belt that could double as a gun holster – where she planned on hiding a small fake pistol to whip out for comedy effect after the ceremony. It wasn't an everyday request, but perfectly doable with a bit of fast stitching and the occasional dollop of cheat glue.

She'd normally be doing this in the fitting room, but, well. It just wasn't big enough – so she was out on the shop floor of Ellen's Empire, crawling around in discarded scraps of material and the stray threads of cotton that always seemed to coat the tiles, no matter how much she swept up.

As she worked, the hoop held over her head, Gaynor rattled on about the reception (200 of their closest friends, including Maggie), and their honeymoon (the Seychelles, not including Maggie), and the fact that she planned to eat her own bodyweight in Terry's Chocolate Orange the minute the dress was off, before she did anything else at all. Tony would undoubtedly be delighted with that schedule.

Maggie couldn't hear everything clearly, and just kept shouting the occasional encouraging sound as she practised inserting the little gun into the holster, and pulling it back out to test its quick draw qualities. Yup. It seemed to be working just fine, and would definitely make for an entertaining photo or seven. Not quite a shotgun wedding, but she got the gag.

As she decided she was finally happy, she slipped the gun out again. It, too, was decorated with faux pearls – and had been filched from a Calamity Jane fancy dress outfit Gaynor had found online. Maggie took one more deep breath before trying to fight her way out again, carefully lifting the hooping, listening to the swish of acres of material, before crawling back out.

At exactly that moment – with her backside inching away, head still submerged in Gaynor's flounce – the doorbell to the shop rang. Perfect timing. She should really have flipped the sign to 'closed'.

Maggie climbed to her feet, wiping multi-coloured threads off the knees of her jeans, and turned to face her visitor. Gaynor giggled, and she realised she was brandishing the fake pistol in his direction.

"Don't shoot! I'll go peacefully!" he said, face creasing into a grin. A grin she recognised. The grin that belonged to the Man from the Park.

Her face already flushed from getting way too up close and personal with Gaynor's stockinged thighs, she tucked a wild lock of her hair behind her ear, and tried not to look embarrassed. There was, she told herself, nothing to be embarrassed about. Certainly, she'd just crawled out from another woman's crotch, and yes, she was pointing a toy gun at him. But he didn't know that she recognised him. That she'd been ruthlessly mocked by her own daughter for leching over him. That several times, often late at night, she'd found herself remembering him – his height, the wide shoulders, the easy way he carried his bulk. The infectious love he'd obviously felt for his toddler son.

The toddler in question was also with him, and staring wide-eyed at the huge dress. Once his mind had processed it, he ambled towards the table that held Maggie's small but perfectly formed Christmas tree. She'd made all the decorations herself with spare white silk and taffeta, and sprinkled them with glitter. It was... tasteful. Definitely a lot more tasteful than the one she had at home, which looked like a drunken elf had vomited a rainbow all over it.

The boy reached out, hands grubby from some chocolatey treat, and the man immediately walked over towards him and gently but firmly pulled him away.

"No, Luca – you have to be decontaminated before you touch anything like this."

The child looked up at him, obviously debating whether he could make a break for it.

"No want show!" he said, defiantly, stamping one wellington-clad foot.

"I know you don't want a shower, but you're gonna get one – just as soon as we're finished here."

He hoisted the little boy up into arms that – Maggie couldn't help but notice – were delightfully big and brawny. She had a momentary flash of him in Russell Crowe's Gladiator outfit and felt her cheeks burn even brighter. She reminded herself that in reality, he was wearing yet another Christmas jumper – this one featuring Santa Claus with a bobble on his hat. He must have a collection of them at home.

"That's okay," she said, walking towards the tree and picking off one of the decorations. "These were made by Christmas pixies. They left a load of them – you can take one with you, if you like?"

The child looked at her, and looked at the sparkling bow she was holding out. Then he looked at the man, eyes big and hopeful. After getting a nod of approval, the boy grabbed it out of her hand as fast as one of those frogs catching a fly on a nature video. Scary reflexes.

"Thank you," said the man. "That's really kind. He'll probably try and eat it, but what the hell...I was wondering if you could help me with a suit that needs altering. I have a Christening to go to, and my own got lost on the 'plane journey over from the States. I got the nearest I could find, but...well, it's a little on the tight side."

Maggie bit back a small gulp, and laid a hand on the Christmas table for support.

"I bet!" piped up Gaynor, with perfect comic timing, "you're the size of the jolly green giant!"

"Not *gween*!" replied Luca, before promptly stuffing the corner of the Christmas ribbon into his chocolate-coated mouth.

"Oh...I see...well, I'm really sorry, but I don't do men..." Maggie stammered, realising as she said it that she might possibly have created the wrong impression. Or, unintentionally, the right one – she hadn't actually done a man in many years. Her friend Sian said she was convinced 'it' had grown over again now, like when you leave your ear-rings out too long. Sian was classy like that.

He raised his eyebrows, his wide mouth managing to somehow smile with the upward tilt of just one corner. Gawd, she thought, he had a gorgeous mouth.

"I mean I don't do men's clothes. Obviously."

"Obviously," he replied, seeming to be quite enjoying her blush-a-thon. "Well, can you recommend anyone? Anyone who does do men?"

"I do men!" said Gaynor, before guffawing like Barbara Windsor after three bottles of Rioja.

Luca joined in, giggling away even if he had no idea what he was laughing at. He really was adorable – if slightly on the terrifying side.

"You could try Lock's, up near Cornmarket. He should be able to help."

He nodded his thanks, and maintained eye contact for just a fraction longer than the circumstances merited. Please leave, she thought, and let my face fade back to its normal shade. But for some reason he wasn't moving – his bulk was between her and the door, making her feel trapped and hot and way too bothered.

He maintained that annoyingly intense eye contact and grinned wickedly at her, as though he knew exactly what she was thinking.

Maggie tried to smile back, aiming for friendly-but-firm, but thought she probably looked a bit like the Elephant Man as she did it. Her insides were going a bit squishy, and there was a strange ringing noise in her ears. She felt like she should say something more, try and at least appear like a normal intelligent human being, but her vocal chords had decided to go on strike. He was just so...shiny. And big. And healthy. There was a kind of glow around him – the Ready Brek boy crossed with GI Joe. For some reason, it made speech completely impossible.

"I need to go doo-doo," said Luca.

At least someone wasn't stuck for words.

Chapter 4

Everything was hurting. His ribs, his face. His leg. Especially his goddamn leg. Marco had played a lot of sports in his life, and been on the receiving end of a lot of injuries, often inflicted by men the size of small SUVs. But nothing had ever quite hurt as much as this. He felt...broken. All over. He'd been well and truly Humpty-Dumptied.

It had all happened so quickly. One minute he was pumping along, listening to the playlist Leah had sent him, mind drifting in and out of the lectures he'd been working on, and the next... wham, bam, thank you ma'am – he was off his bike, and lying in the freezing snow wheezing for breath and wanting to cry like a great big baby. With the sounds of Aerosmith's *Love In An Elevator* still very inappropriately bouncing around his brain. It was probably all their fault – rock music must have made him cycle too fast.

And now, on top of it all, on top of all of the pain and the confusion and the damn cold, there was this crazy woman – screaming at him so loud his ears were starting to hurt as well. She was definitely screaming louder than Steven Tyler had been a few minutes earlier.

She was crouched next to him, kneeling in the snow, and shaking him by the shoulders. Each little tug sent even more excruciating pain ricocheting down his left leg like an electric shock. The worst thing was he couldn't even understand properly what she was saying – he was probably in shock. Or in concussion. Or in limbo, as the Big Guy decided whether he was going to get sent upstairs to the celestial choirs or downstairs to the red hot pokers. Dead In An Elevator.

Even that, he thought, trying to focus on the words flying out of her mouth, would be better than this torment. He blinked a couple of times, clenched his fists together so tight he could feel nails cutting into his palms, and stared up at her. Come on, man, he told himself. Get a grip.

He could hear the sound of sirens wailing in the background, and hoped that help was on its way. That there'd be morphine soon. Oblivion. Even if it did come with red hot pokers. He just needed to hold on for a little while longer; man up until he was whisked away in the back of the truck with the paramedics.

"Yeah, yeah…okay…stop shaking me, for Christ's sake!" he managed to say, "it hurts like hell!"

Abruptly the woman dropped her hold on his shoulders, raising her trembling, blue-tinged fingers into the air with a gesture of surrender. Her eyes were bright green; filled with shining, unshed tears. Wild loops of red hair were tufting out of her cycling helmet, creating a fuzzy auburn halo around her whole head. She looked… crazed. And vaguely familiar.

"I'm sorry!" she said, leaning in close to his face. "But where's the baby? Where's Luca?"

"He's not here, okay? He's fine! I'm…not fine! Didn't you wonder if I might have had a spinal injury before you started shaking me like that, you crazy woman? I could be paralysed for life!"

She fell back onto her bottom, relief flashing across her face, the tears finally falling. He saw a spasm of pain cloud her expression and she wiggled around in the snow, trying to find a more comfortable position. He recognised that pose. Bruised coccyx. He'd been knocked on his own ass enough times to spot the symptoms. He'd actually feel sorry for her, if it wasn't for the searing agony of his own. He tried to move his leg a fraction of an inch; was relieved when it responded – he wasn't paralysed for life, after all – but unprepared for how much it was going to hurt.

Marco let out a scream, then bit his lip so hard he felt tasted blood. Jeez. This was not good. Not good at all.

The woman he'd collided with leaned forward, and he recoiled as much as he could. For all he knew she was going to whip out a red hot poker any second now.

"Hey – don't start shaking me again, okay, lady? Just...back off!"

She nodded, but stayed at his side. He felt her icy fingers crawl into his, and her other hand gently stroked stray hair back from his forehead.

"I'm sorry," she said again, her voice now low and soothing and not as generally all-out terrifying as before. "I saw the baby seat on the back. You came into my shop yesterday, and I thought, well...I thought the worst."

He held tight onto her fingers. She was even colder than him. So cold that every tear that fell threatened to freeze on her eyelashes. She had terrific eyes...huge, clear, the colour of dark green grass. Eyes that went with the pale, freckled skin, the long, deep red hair. Once he'd mentally removed the cycling helmet, it came back to him: it was the woman from the little place with the dresses in the window. The seamstress with the smile and the toy gun. The chick who'd given Luca that Christmas bow he loved so much. Wow. Small world, he thought, as another wave of pain crashed through him.

It explained her reactions, at least. Who gave a damn about a big oaf like him if there was a two-year-old cutie pie on the loose? If the roles had been reversed, he'd have shaken her too.

"It's all right. He's safe. Now, tell me...does that leg look right to you? It sure as hell doesn't feel right."

She glanced down, and tried hard to hide her involuntary shudder at what she saw.

"It looks just fine. Nothing a few stitches won't fix." And possibly a few metal plates and a skin graft, thought Maggie, while trying to smile reassuringly. It was a hideous mangled mess of jeans and banged up flesh. She hadn't stared too long in case she started to notice any bright white bone that really shouldn't be visible at all.

"'Kay," he replied, strengthening his grip on her fingers. "I'll take your word for it. You know all about stitches. Listen, keep hold of me, all right? My ID's in my pocket. My phone's in there too; look for numbers for Rob and Leah and get the hospital dudes to call them, will you?"

"Don't be daft," she said, "you'll be able to call them yourself soon."

"Nah," he replied, his head lolling back down into the snow, listing to one side. "I think I'm gonna pass out now. And I think I'm going to enjoy it."

Chapter 5

The woman who was handing Maggie a coffee was a good few inches shorter than her. Probably a good few years younger than her. And definitely a whole lot more pregnant than her.

She was also, Maggie thought, heart-breakingly pretty. Blonde hair, tied up in a loose pony. Gorgeous skin. Huge, amber-coloured eyes. Five foot nothing and about ready to pop.

She lowered herself slowly down into the plastic chair next to Maggie, huffing and puffing as she sat, assuming the 'bowling ball between legs' pose beloved of heavily pregnant women the world over.

"I'll be needing one of those soon," she said to Maggie, pointing down at the inflatable cushion she was perched on. "After Luca was born I didn't sit down for three days – just lay on my big wobbly belly, demanding caviar and champagne, while I watched reruns of America's Next Top Model and hated all the thin girls!"

Maggie gave her a half smile, not sure if she was joking or not.

"Joking," she said, clearing the matter up. "But I was pretty sore, and I still hate all the thin girls. You know how it is. Do you? Do you have kids?"

"One daughter," replied Maggie, transferring the scalding hot coffee into the other hand to avoid adding third degree burns to her bruised coccyx. "But she's 18 now. And one of the thin girls."

The woman – Leah, she now knew, Marco Cavelli's sister in law – did the usual surprised double take. Refreshingly, she didn't even try and hide it. She didn't seem the sort of person who was easily embarrassed. She was just too comfortable in her own skin to even bother.

"Wow," she said, sipping her own hot chocolate and grimacing at the taste, the heat, or possibly the combination of the two. "You started early. High school sweetheart or too much swigging cider in the park at the weekend?"

Maggie laughed out loud – spilling Nescafe's finest on her jeans as she did. She'd hit very close to the mark. Maybe she'd had a misspent youth as well.

"A little bit of both, actually," she replied. "Seemed like a disaster at the time, but...well, it wasn't. It was the best thing that ever happened to me."

Leah nodded, her blonde pony bobbing vigorously. "I know exactly what you mean. Luca was something of a happy accident as well, and he's—"

"Adorable," finished Maggie for her.

"Yes. I'd say I was biased, but it's quite obviously a statement of objective fact – he is the most adorable little boy who ever walked the planet. Although he's not exactly delighted right now – when we got your call we were about to head back up to Scotland with him. Instead, he's stuck back in Marco's flat, being looked after by his landlady, who he regards as one step down the moral ladder from Cruella de Vil. The landlady's looked after him before and...well, let's just say it took the mention of ambulances and emergency operations to persuade her to do it again!"

Maggie had been at the hospital for the last three hours. She'd drunk approximately fifteen of these coffees, in their finger-killingly thin plastic containers. She'd had her arse X-rayed. She'd been poked and prodded by a boy of about 12 who claimed he was a doctor but

23

had to be lying. And she'd been given two paracetamol and an inflatable cushion to sit on. Her precious first edition was crumpled and soggy and stuffed in her backpack, she'd never got to her chocolate tiffin, and all things considered, it had been the Worst Day Off Ever.

Still, at least she was in one piece. Which was more than could be said for Marco. He'd been whisked away by the doctors once they got here, and had been too doped up to talk once the paramedics arrived. So Maggie had lingered in the family room as she waited for Doogie Howser to tell her what she already knew – she had a sore bum – and used Marco's phone to call his family.

Rob – his brother – was on voicemail, but Leah had picked up straight away, answering in a fake American accent with 'what gives, stud-in-law?'.

There'd been a fairly awkward conversation where Maggie explained what had happened, Luca squawking away in the background, and a slightly stunned pause where Leah finally connected the words 'Marco', 'accident', and 'hospital'.

They'd arrived an hour later, and Leah had come straight through to find Maggie, while her husband went to 'harangue the living daylights out of the staff', as Leah put it.

Since then, the two women had been sitting together, sipping hot beverages, and making small talk as Maggie wriggled around on her inflatable cushion. There was a small fake Christmas tree on one table, and a few dusty drapes of tinsel over the doorframe. It was one of the least festive places she'd ever been, and she was desperate to just get home, take more pain killers, and soak her nether regions in hot water and Radox. Hopefully Ellen would be in later, and they'd have a fun old night applying ibuprofen gel, eating Chinese takeaway, and swapping war stories.

Luca, it turned out, wasn't Marco's son at all. He was super uncle, not super dad. He'd been staying here with Marco – who was delivering a guest lecture at the Law Institute – while Leah and Rob had a few days together in their cottage in Scotland.

"Though technically it's not ours," said Leah. "It belongs to a midget called Morag. Which I know sounds ridiculous because I look like I still need one of those plastic steps toddlers use to reach the bathroom sink, but Morag is both a midget and a thin girl. I've never forgiven her for making me feel fat the first time I stayed there, and tried to squeeze into her clothes. I only had a wedding dress with me at the time..."

Maggie raised her eyebrows, about to ask the obvious question. And also to ask what kind of wedding dress, purely out of professional curiosity.

"Long story," said Leah, grinning. "Let's just say it ended with loads of fabulous sex, me moving to Chicago with Rob, and eventually with Luca arriving on the scene to turn all our lives upside down. And now, with little Bella here," she finished, rubbing her vast tummy.

"It's a girl?" Maggie asked, feeling the familiar combination of broodiness, regret and several shades of envy flood over her. She recognised its arrival, and tried to mentally scoop it back into the bitter little box where it belonged.

"We don't know for sure," replied Leah, "but I'm insisting that the universe provides me with at least one other person who doesn't pee on the toilet seat."

"Just wait until she's a teenager and you're sharing a bathroom cabinet with her," said Maggie, recalling the disaster zone that was Ellen's shelf back at home. "You might yearn for a bit of pee on the toilet seat."

"Ha! That may be very true...oh, look, here's my lord and master – he'll have news for us..."

Leah dumped her hot chocolate cup on the table, and dragged herself to her feet as quickly and gracefully as it was possible for one human being containing another human being to do.

The man who had entered the room walked towards her, scooping his vertically challenged wife into his arms and squeezing her tight enough to produce a little 'eek!'. Leah rested her head against his chest for a moment, and Maggie could almost feel the relief flowing from her.

She'd been so chatty, appeared so relaxed, that Maggie had been starting to wonder if she was worried about Marco at all. Now, she realised, she had been. With this man to lean on, she suddenly looked small and scared and less larger-than-life. Like she was finally able to relax.

Leah reached up and placed her hands on either side of Rob's face, planting a big wet kiss on his lips, before disentangling herself and leading him over to Maggie.

"Maggie, meet Rob," she said. "Rob, meet Maggie. No, don't try and get up – think of your poor bottom!"

Maggie did as she was told and stayed seated. Her poor bottom was indeed protesting. Instead, she looked up at Marco's brother, and despite the unpleasant circumstances, couldn't help but like what she saw. He was just as tall – maybe less brawny – and had the same dark, wavy hair. His eyes were brown, not hazel, but the resemblance was strong. Strong enough to make her blush as she recalled some of the less than chaste thoughts she'd had about his twin over the last few days.

"Hi Maggie," he said, squatting down in front of her so he was on eye level. "Thanks so much for everything you've done. He's back in recovery – they were able to reset the bone without surgery, and the docs say he'll be fine; it wasn't anything too complicated. I just spoke to him for a couple of minutes. He's pretty high, so I'm not sure what this means, but he said to tell you he surrenders – don't shoot him, don't shake him, and don't scream at him."

"Oooh," said Leah with a giggle, "that all sounds very interesting! I thought you two didn't know each other? How've you managed to fit all that in?"

"We don't know each other," replied Maggie, finishing off the coffee and urging her red cheeks to fade back down to acceptable levels. Having Rob so up close and personal wasn't really helping on that point – he had that same tanned, fit, healthy glow that she'd noticed in his brother. It wasn't really fair to womankind.

"But...well, we've crossed paths. Until we were on the same path, that is. Then it all got a bit nasty. Is he all right?"

"Yes, Rob," added Leah, "will he ever play the violin again?"

"Probably not with his left leg," he answered, dashing his wife a white-toothed grin. "But he'll be okay. You want to go see him? Both of you?"

Maggie started to protest – it was, in all honesty, the last thing she wanted to do. She was throbbing in unmentionable places – and not in a good way. Her clothes were still damp. Her hair was so big she might not even make it through the door frame. She needed to get home, back to comfort and calm and safety – and away from dangerously sexy American men and their heart-wrenchingly pregnant wives.

Leah listened to her spluttering, and fixed her with a no-nonsense amber stare.

"Of course you want to see him, Maggie," she said firmly. "Why ever else have you been hanging round here for the last three hours? It certainly wasn't for the coffee."

Chapter 6

"I could hire a nurse," said Rob, frowning at his still doped brother.

"Well, make it a hot one..." Marco mumbled in reply, his eyes slowly focusing on Maggie, who was lurking in the doorway, leaning on the frame and looking decidedly uncomfortable being there at all. His eyes were still a little fuzzy, and she looked like a giant blob of red hair stuck on top of a body.

"No – we're going to find the nastiest, meanest, ugliest nurse in Britain," added Leah, who was sitting at the end of the bed looking at his medical chart. "It says right here that you need someone over 70 with facial warts."

"Hey – I have a generous spirit when it comes to women," answered Marco, struggling with the remote control to his bed until he was semi-upright. "I could find that hot. I could find anything hot right now, I'm on so many drugs. Maggie – that's your name right? Come on in. How's your ass?"

She walked slowly into the room, trying to ignore Leah's little snigger at the question, and sat carefully down on the spare chair next to him. He was wearing a puke-green hospital gown that was way too small for him, and he certainly wasn't glowing any more. He was hooked up to various beepy machines, and had a drip attached to his arm by one of those horrible spiky things that always made her cringe. She could see the outline of his plaster-cast leg beneath the sheet, which was equally cringey. The crash hadn't been her fault – but she still felt guilty.

"My 'ass' is wonderful, thank you," she replied, placing one hand on the edge of the bed. He quickly covered it with one of his own, luckily not the one with the spiky thing in it. "How's yours?"

"It's hanging out of this gown, for one thing...hey, Maggie? Thanks for sticking around. Thanks for calling these guys. And I'm so sorry about the accident. I'm glad it's me who ended up here, not you."

"So am I," she said, linking her fingers into his and giving them a quick squeeze. She'd been aiming for friendly and reassuring, but found herself in such a tight grip that it started to feel entirely different. Maggie tried to pull her hand away, but he held on, and winked at her as she struggled. His eyes were clouded with pain and drugs, but they still managed to have enough sparkle to make her tummy contract. She remembered those eyes so well from his visit to the shop. The way they looked at her for just a little bit too long; the way they'd made her feel exposed and cornered and just a little bit gooey inside.

It wasn't just the eyes, of course. The face was pretty gorgeous as well. The wide smiling mouth; the cheekbones. The ridiculously impressive arms bulking out of the green gown. It was very inappropriate to notice such things at the side of a hospital bed – but she wasn't blind. Or dead. Just very, very...jittery. Yes. That would be the word. Not horny at all – that would be sick, under the circumstances, and she wasn't sure she'd recognise it even if it was true. She was just...jittery. In some very strange places.

"Maybe *you* could be my nurse," said Marco, grinning at her, a flash of brilliance on a pain-wracked face.

"She's not ugly enough," interjected Leah, looking up from charts she couldn't even understand.

Hmm, Leah thought. Medical charts, I don't understand. But the way Marco's looking at Maggie, and the way Maggie's trying so hard not to look back at him? That, I *do* understand. Leah switched her narrow-eyed gaze over to Rob, and saw from the one quizzically raised eyebrow that he'd noticed too. For anyone who knew Marco, it was hard to miss.

Leah snapped the file shut, and leaned back in the chair. She loved it when a plan came together. Now she just had to convince everyone else she was Hannibal Smith, and get started on that imaginary cigar.

Chapter 7

Maggie's living room had been transformed into a scene from *Casualty*. Normally spacious, with high ceilings and a huge bay window that flooded it with light, the whole space was now dominated by a recliner chair and a hospital-type bed.

A hospital-type bed that Leah was busy decorating with tinsel, looping the strands around the rails and making small coo-ing noises as she stood back and took in the overall effect.

"What do you think?" she said, glancing up at Maggie, and gesturing at the bed in a 'ta-da!' gesture.

I think, said Maggie to herself – completely silently – that I've made some kind of terrible mistake. I think I want my house back. I think I'm just not a nice enough person to do this.

"I think," she said out loud, "that I feel a very large gin and tonic coming on."

"Ha! I am so jealous...just wait til I've popped this one out, and I'll be back to visit – me and you will go and paint the town red, Maggie!"

Maggie couldn't help but smile at the idea. There was something about Leah – something infectiously happy – that was hard to resist. In fact, it was all because of that infectious quality that her beautiful Victorian cottage living room had been hi-jacked at all. That and – just possibly, she had to concede – the fact that she did give at least a teeny tiny Christmas fig about what happened to Marco Cavelli. The Hot Papa from the Park. The Man with the Tux. The idiot who'd crashed his way into her life – and now, apparently, taken it over.

It was five days since the accident, and two days since Leah had turned up at Ellen's Empire bearing a huge bouquet of white roses, and an equally huge box of very posh chocolates. Rob had come in first, opening the door with its customary jingle, and they'd found Maggie sweeping up. As usual. Specifically she was trying to get at a card of hooks and eyes she'd dropped behind the sewing machine.

There was a tape measure draped around her neck, and her hair was swept up into a wild bun. Tiny strands of ivory cotton were stuck like linty limpets to the front of her black T-shirt, and she'd tied a ribbon made of discarded satin around her wrist to remind her to buy milk on the way home. It was her version of writing a note on the back of her hand.

"Wow," said Leah, smiling at her, "you look like Cinderella."

"And you're my fairy godmother?" replied Maggie, propping the brush up against the wall and walking forward to take the gifts. She instinctively sniffed at the flowers, and was rewarded with a deep, decadent whoosh of rosy gorgeousness going up her nose. One of her favourite smells ever.

"Depends on your point of view," added Rob, looking around the ultra-feminine shop with the air of a sea creature stranded in the Sahara Desert. "If you listen to her long enough, the wicked stepmother starts coming more to mind..."

Leah made a fake-outraged harrumph and poked him in the stomach, just as the door to the fitting room opened. Out of it walked Lucy Allsop, wearing one of the most beautiful dresses Maggie had ever worked on.

Lucy was tall and slender with deep brown hair and sunkissed skin, and her dress fitted her like...well, like it had been made just for her. Which it had, with a great deal of care. The A-line shape skimmed over her slim waist, a v-neck hinted at curves but stayed within the boundaries of classy, and the whole gown was covered in lace applique. The arms and the back were made of sheer lace that gave it all a vintage feel, and Lucy's colouring made her one of those rare brides who could pull off pure white without a hint of anaemia.

She looked absolutely stunning – and also a little stunned, as she emerged into a room to be confronted by a heavily pregnant woman who'd need the world's biggest frock, and her devastatingly attractive husband.

"Oh my gosh!" said Leah, breaking the ice and scurrying over towards her, "you look completely gorgeous – like a foxy Kate Middleton!"

"Umm...thank you?" replied Lucy, running her hands nervously over the lace. "You don't think it's a bit...tight?"

Maggie's heart sank at the words. She'd heard variations on them many times before. Always from jittery brides who secretly wanted nothing more in the world than a six pack of Wagon Wheels, terrified that they'd made some terrible couture cock-up, freaking out about the whole thing. It was rarely about the dress itself –more about the impending life-changing event. She might be a dressmaker, but she also sidelined as life coach, best friend and anxiety management expert.

Lucy, in particular, was under pressure – from her own parents, from in-laws, from the huge wedding that had grown from a family gathering into a huge, sprawling mass of a thing. She'd completely lost control of it all, and several of the recent fittings had been accompanied by tears, and on one occasion a bottle of emergency Prosecco.

"No, no, no! It's perfect – you're perfect – everything about it is perfect, and you're going to have the most perfect day!" gushed

Leah, looking at Rob for back-up. Leah's personality was huge, but Maggie had noticed how often she involved her husband in her conversations – he seemed to be her other half in pretty much every way.

"You look wonderful," said Rob on cue, the American accent making Lucy's eyebrows pop up a fraction of an inch. "And whoever the lucky guy is, he's going to be lost for words when he sees you walking down the aisle."

Lucy stared at him for a moment, a slow blush managing to creep its way up her cheeks, and nodded.

"Good. That was the idea. Maggie, I'll just go back in and try on some of the jewellery, okay?"

"Lovely – I'll be in in a few minutes to help you out of it. And they're right Lucy – you look fantastic. You and the dress are both breathtaking."

Lucy gave her a small, sad smile, then flicked one more glance in the direction of Rob – tall, dark, glamorous and pretty hard not to look at – before retreating back into the fitting room, apparently reassured. Phew, thought Maggie. Good save.

She laid the flowers and chocolates down next to the Christmas tree – the one Luca had been so fascinated with – and walked back to her unexpected guests.

"Thanks for that," she said, tucking her always-straying red hair back behind her ears. "Lucy's had a hard time. And the brides... well, they get nervous."

"I remember," replied Leah. "I felt exactly the same. The lady who made my dress – second time round, the first dress was as much of a disaster as the wedding I never quite made it to – was near to a breakdown by the time I'd finished with all my whinging – I was so desperate for it all to be perfect."

Maggie had the bare bones of their story now, told in fits and starts by Leah, Rob and his brother: Leah had been all set for a fairy tale wedding of her own, on Christmas Eve three years ago, until she found her fiancé in a deeply compromising position with one of the bridesmaids. She'd driven away in horror, suffered a very serendipitous vehicle malfunction, and ended up stranded in a snow storm outside Rob's cottage in Scotland – still wearing the dress. The rest, thought Maggie, taking in the giant tummy and the magnificently happy woman who wielded it, was very romantic history.

"You'd have looked perfect to me if you'd walked into the room wearing a clown outfit, with a big red nose and huge shoes," said Rob, giving her a smile that would have made every woman in a three-mile radius melt a little inside. "Even if you'd sprayed my face with water from a fake flower."

God. They were just so in love, thought Maggie. In a way she'd never, ever experienced. The irony wasn't lost on her – the way she made her living creating beautiful dresses for women about to marry their great loves. She'd never been married. Never even been in love. Never experienced that contented glow that Leah radiated, enjoying a pregnancy rather than being ashamed of it; with a deeply committed man beside her side every step of the way, instead of an embarrassed and terrified 17-year-old kid who was doing his best but was really still a child himself. It was like looking into a different world.

"How is he?" asked Maggie, a little abruptly. She needed to break the spell. Stop feeling sorry for herself. Help Lucy out of the dress. Go and buy milk. Continue to go about a life that might not be all hearts and flowers, but was perfectly satisfactory, thank you very much.

"Good," replied Leah, finally dragging her eyes away from her husband. "He's coming out in a couple of days. We've got to head back up to Scotland soon to carry on arranging the Christening, and hopefully he'll be able to follow us up in time for Christmas

Eve. He just needs a bit of TLC between now and then and he'll be fine – the doctor's say for the first three weeks, he should try and stay put and recuperate so he's ready to travel. In fact, that's kind of why we're here..."

And somehow – from the start of that conversation – Maggie had found her life and her home turned completely upside down and inside out.

At first she'd said no. And at second, and at third, and at fourth. But somehow, somehow, she'd been convinced. Leah's approach had been emotional, predictably enough. Marco didn't really know anyone here; he needed company, and – the big finale – she, Leah, heavily preggers and distressed as she was, just wouldn't feel safe leaving him in the hands of a stranger. If it wasn't for the impending arrival of Baby Bella, and needing to look after Luca, and the Christening, she'd have stayed herself – and she couldn't bear the thought of poor, lonely Marco being abandoned to some unfamiliar Nurse Ratched figure.

Maggie had listened to it all, knowing she was being manipulated, but grudgingly admiring the way it was being done. Then Rob had started in, with a lot more common sense. It would only be for a few of weeks. They could pay for anything she needed – equipment, extra care if necessary, a vehicle big enough for the wheelchair. Marco wasn't used to being laid low, and was likely to need a firm hand – he'd be trying to do way too much too soon, and he already knew Maggie. Felt responsible for what had happened. Would be less likely to ignore her advice than he would hired help. They could also compensate her financially if it affected her work, pay her whatever the going rate was.

It was at that point she'd held up her hands, accidentally throwing the tape measure over one shoulder, and said: "Enough! I've heard enough. Leah, lovely as you are, I can recognise bullshit when I hear it. And Rob – I'm not after money. I only have one final dress to sort out before Christmas so I won't be losing work. The issue here is...well, I have a daughter at home, I have a father who's not as young as he was. I have responsibilities. I have a life of my own."

At least some of that was a lie, she knew even as she said it. Ellen was way too busy to need her, and her dad was 68, fit as a fiddle, and had a better social calendar than both of them put together. As for her own life...she could pretty much jot down her engagements on the back of a matchbox, once she removed work. So, what was the real reason? Did she even have the answer herself?

"I'm really sorry for what happened to Marco, but I'm not sure I'm the right person to be helping him out in his hour of need. I'm not a nanny – I'm a dressmaker. And what makes you think he'll want to stay with me anyway? He was looking for a hot nurse last time I saw him! What makes you think he'll listen to a word I'll say?"

Rob and Leah looked at each other, and to Maggie's surprise it was Rob who replied.

"I just have a feeling about it," he said. "That he'll get better quicker if he's with someone he knows – if he's with you. And I've learned over the years to trust my instincts. I'm asking you to trust them as well."

Chapter 8

And so it had come to pass, against all her better judgment, that Marco Cavelli was to be her unexpected houseguest for the next few weeks.

Maggie had half hoped that Ellen would object, and give her the perfect excuse to say no – but once her daughter had stopped laughing, she was all in favour of the idea.

"It'll give you something to do," she'd said, "other than drink gin and watch Christmas cooking shows. Last year's obsession with goose fat still haunts me. Now you can drink gin and watch him instead. Invite Sian round, and those women from the park. It'll be like a Chippendales' party. I'm fine with it as long as he stays out of my stuff."

Her dad, Paddy, had been just as annoyingly supportive.

"It's the Christian thing to do, love," he'd said, "a stranger in need and all that. Especially at this time of year. Beside, it'll keep you busy, won't it?"

Both responses had highlighted one very unpleasant fact to Maggie: that her nearest and dearest obviously saw her as a sad, lonely being floating through life with nothing to occupy her other than work and them. The even more unpleasant fact was that they might just be right.

She'd always been secretly proud of how she'd coped with the challenges life had thrown at her. Losing her mum when she was

38

14. Getting pregnant not that long after. Abandoning her hope to go to University when she chose to keep the baby. The trauma of the birth and the surgery that followed it. The long, sometimes difficult years that had come after.

She'd raised her child – who had, despite her acid tongue, turned out beautifully – and had managed to make a living from what had always been a hobby. She'd kept them fed and housed and happy – mostly all on her own. She'd learned to be independent and smart and strong, looking after her dad when he needed it and making sure Ellen had everything a girl could wish for.

But now the landscape of her life was changing. Paddy was well out of his dark days, the days when he viewed life through the bottom of a glass, and Ellen...well, Ellen was starting to create the landscape of her own life. Which was good – it was the way it was supposed to be; you raise a child well enough, confident enough, capable enough, and you get rewarded by seeing them fly the nest. It was the natural rhythm of life – but one that perhaps, Maggie had to acknowledge, she hadn't been quite prepared for.

Caring for Marco might be ever so slightly terrifying – but it would indeed keep her busy.

Leah had finally left, having hustled and bustled her way through the house making sure everything was 'just perfect' – which mainly seemed to involve adding Christmas decorations, riding up and down on the recliner chair while making small excited noises, and stocking the fridge with Marco's favourite beer. She'd headed back up to Scotland with Rob and Luca, full of promises to stay in touch, giving Maggie a massive hug on the doorstep before she disappeared off into the snow.

The snow that was still falling – coating the front garden like icing on a very large cake, where it remained, pure and untouched. Not so long ago Ellen would have been out there making snowballs and ambushing passing postmen. Now, she was out at the pub, saying a fond farewell to her super-posh boyfriend Jacob and drinking cider.

Maggie looked out of the window. Looked at her watch. Almost 6pm. He was due any minute, and she had no idea what she was going to do with him. The main living room was now kitted out for him to use, and a nurse was going to come every morning to help him with his 'personal care'. Even the words made her blush, so she hadn't pondered that one too closely. There was a TV, she had DVDs, and there was a downstairs loo – which he'd definitely need if he drank all that beer Leah had bought. The second living room – usually draped with fabric samples, patterns and bridal magazine cuttings – had been tidied and cleared so that Maggie had her own space to retreat to.

Upstairs – due to the annoying but convenient broken leg – would be completely out of bounds for Marco. Probably a good thing – the only man Maggie had ever lived with had been her own father, and Ellen had never lived with one at all. He'd probably faint at the sight of their hoards of undies, make-up, and never-put-away tampon boxes. There'd never been any need to man-proof that part of the house, and Maggie was glad there still wasn't. She remained convinced that one puff of testosterone would result in the whole bathroom exploding.

A few minutes after six, a car drove up outside. It was one of those boxy van-type things, and Maggie knew it had been hired for her to use, to ferry Marco around if he needed it. Her own car – a little Fiat 500 – probably wasn't big enough for him even without the broken leg.

She watched as a man in uniform walked to the back, and pulled out a folded wheelchair. He set it up, then walked round to the side of the van and slid the doors open. Marco immediately tried to stand up, using the frame of the car for support, and she looked on as the nurse told him off, insisting instead that he waited until he could help ease him into the chair.

Marco's face as he did it was a picture of frustration and clenched anger. Maggie bit back a smile – looked like Rob was definitely right about one thing. He was indeed going to be a difficult patient.

She jumped off the window seat and ran round to the front door, opening it wide. Luckily there were no steps, it opened right out onto the path, and she stood there with chattering teeth as her new ward was wheeled towards her, the chair making parallel tracks in the snow as it moved.

He looked a lot better than the last time she saw him, which probably wouldn't have been difficult. The tanned skin had regained its healthy glow; his poor face was starting to heal, and he was wearing loose-fitting sweat pants rather than a puke green hospital gown. His left leg was in plaster and propped upright, and he had a laptop case resting on his knees.

His eyes met hers as he was pushed up the pathway, and he gave her a little lopsided grin that added to the goosebumps. She had the sneaky feeling this man could be coated head to toe in plaster and still make her tummy feel odd.

The nurse came to a stop outside the door, his face creased with a massive frown. It had clearly been a fun ride from the hospital for both of them.

"So," said Marco, looking up at her, "we meet again. Any chance of a beer? My grandma back here refused to stop on the way."

Chapter 9

Jeez, thought Marco, as he listened to that damn nurse go through his 'patient aftercare checklist' for the third time. The man needed to take a chill pill. He'd gone on and on and on. Explaining the meds, explaining the chair, explaining the warning signs. When to up the dosage. When to call the doctor. When to bring him to the emergency room. He talked about him as though he wasn't there, wasn't sitting right in front of him, wasn't ready to stagger straight out of this nifty gadget of a recliner and whack him over the head with his crutches.

He'd had broken bones before. It was no big deal – it hurt like hell, but he'd heal. This guy, though – he was talking to Maggie as though she was about to take on the care of whole platoon of war veterans. The poor woman was looking more flustered by the second as she tried to take it all in.

He hadn't even wanted to come here. He understood that Leah and Rob needed to leave, but he saw no reason why he couldn't have simply gone back to his own flat. He'd have been far more comfortable with some hired help. Then, if the mood took him, he could swear, curse, bully, and generally misbehave with no consequences at all other than a mild dose of self-loathing afterwards.

He couldn't behave like that with Maggie – it just wasn't in him. Considering the fact that he'd only met her twice – and that on one of those occasions he was distracted by the business of going unconscious – he cared just a little bit too much about what she thought.

Even when he was lying in the hospital bed doped up on morphine, he'd been concerned about her. Worried about her injury. Mildly embarrassed that she was seeing him flat out and vulnerable. It wasn't exactly how he'd planned to see her again.

That first time, in the wedding dress store, he'd felt how nervous she was around him. Maybe she was like that with everyone – or maybe it was just him. He didn't know, but the effect was the same: it brought out his inner he-man. Made him feel strangely protective towards her; made him want to wrap his arms around her and keep her from the rest of the world.

It had been a strange mix of physical attraction and her attitude – a mix that made him want to both hide her away and, if he was honest, torment her a little bit himself.

The women he usually socialised with didn't have that effect on him. They were usually successful, tough, professional women who used him with as much carefree attention as he used them. Friends with benefits – shallow but satisfying.

In fact the only other woman who had ever made him feel that protective before was Leah – back in those awful, messy days in Chicago, when Rob was behaving like a grade A ass towards her. It felt like a million years ago now, but it had been hard – seeing his brother's pain plunge them all into a black hole of emotional hell.

He'd felt protective towards Leah – but in the way he always imagined a big brother would feel towards a little sis. This was different. His first thought when he met Maggie had been that she was a looker, without even knowing it. His second had been that she came across a little bit shy, a little bit scared. His third had been less wholesome – he'd started to wonder, as they chatted over Luca's bouncing head, how much fun it would be to see what would happen if he pushed, if he provoked; if he managed to coax out some of that fire redheads were supposed to have.

So he'd flirted, made eye contact, lingered there a few moments more than he should have – just to see what might happen. To see if she felt any of that attraction at all, or if it was all on his side. He wasn't arrogant, but he didn't struggle with women – and this one intrigued him right up until the point where Luca's toilet habits had interrupted. He needed to have a word with his nephew about mentioning doo-doo in front of hot women. It just wasn't cool.

He'd thought about making up some excuse to see her again. He was in Oxford for the next few weeks anyway, and it'd be nice to have some company. Especially company that was tall and curvy and had crazy red hair you could imagine spread out all over a pillow.

But before he even had time to consider doing that, fate had stepped in – and he found himself reduced to a pile of rubble in front of the woman he'd been hoping to impress. Once a chick's seen you in a hospital gown, he suspected, there's no going back – you can never be alpha male again…and now, thanks to Leah and Rob's insistence, here he was. Sitting in her shabby chic front room, being treated like a naughty child by Nurse Attila the Hun.

"She gets it," he said, interrupting the nurse mid flow. "She's not an idiot – she gets it. We have the meds. We have the numbers. Now for God's sake, get lost, will you?"

Both the nurse and Maggie stared at him, looking shocked and horror-struck in the way only the English can at bare-faced rudeness – even when it is deserved.

Maggie frowned at him, her knuckles whitening as she clutched the typed-up contact list a little too tightly.

"Don't be so rude," she said, "or there'll be no beer before bed time for you, Mr Cavelli."

She turned back to the nurse, who had started recommending yet again that the patient be given no access to alcohol in his current condition, and started guiding him towards the door. Marco was sure she'd had enough too, but she was just dealing with it a whole lot better than him. He let out a little sigh as they both disappeared off into the corridor.

He *had* been rude. It wasn't called for. He was just...frustrated. Pissed off. Feeling helpless and tired and in more than a little pain. He was used to calling the shots, to being in charge. To the cut and thrust of his work as an attorney. To a full and active life full of sports and friends and women and drinking a beer whenever the hell he wanted to. Being passive really didn't suit him, and now he felt embarrassed at the way he'd reacted. Embarrassed that Maggie had seen him turn into a jackass within minutes of entering her home.

God, he thought, it was going to be a long few weeks. Physical torment, forced inactivity, and some strange compunction to be on his best behaviour around this woman. He felt like crying – but there was no way he could. He was sure Maggie was stressed enough without having to console a wailing wuss as well.

He heard the front door close, and watched as the nurse walked carefully down the snow-coated path. He was on his phone – probably reporting him to the Bad Patient Police – then through the gate and away. The lucky bastard was undoubtedly going to head to the nearest pub to drown his sorrows.

He listened as Maggie closed the door, then to her footsteps coming back down the hallway. There was a pause, then she walked into the room and looked at him with a small frown, hands on her hips.

"How are you feeling?" she finally asked, after a moment of silence.

"In all honesty, like complete shit," he replied.

"Good. Because you're acting like one as well. I know this is difficult – for both of us. I know we're both probably wondering why we went along with this ridiculous plan at all. And I know you're probably feeling frustrated, and in pain. But we've got to find a way to make the best of it. It won't be for long – you'll get better, and we can both go back to our real lives just in time for Christmas. Until then, let's at least try and pretend this isn't completely weird. Deal?"

It was pretty much the longest speech he'd heard from her. Her body language, her eyes, her expression – they were all different than before. The little mouse had gone – all because he'd made her angry. Good to know, he thought, realising that he was kind of enjoying being told off by her. Pervert.

"It's a deal," he said. "I'm sorry. I was being a jerk. I'm not used to sitting around feeling weak, you know?"

"I can imagine," she replied, her green eyes skimming over his not-usually-weak body in a way that definitely suggested more than a care-giving interest. She seemed to realise what she was doing, and reined herself in with an almost physical jolt.

"Right. You sit tight, Marco. I'll go and get you a beer. I think I need one too."

Chapter 10

Two hours later, Marco was in his bed, propped upright, and Maggie was on the recliner, legs tucked beneath her.

They'd navigated a few potential problems – like him getting into the loo on his own after Maggie wheeled him to the door; him refusing to take his meds until she threatened to kick him in the shin, and arguing over who was paying for the take-away pizza. And somehow, she'd felt a whole lot more settled once he'd agreed to clamber up into bed – he was a big presence, and it felt a lot more acceptable to have this large man in her territory once he was tucked away under a blanket.

Now, after a couple of beers, they'd relaxed enough in each other's company to simply talk. Maggie had forgotten to switch the lights on or draw the curtains, and the room was bathed in the glow of the moonlight, the glittering Christmas tree and the flickering images of the muted TV.

He'd told her about his job and his life in the States; about losing his own father to a heart attack; about the death of Rob's first wife and the turmoil that followed. The way the whole family had suffered until Leah came on the scene and saved the bunch of them. She'd told him about Ellen, and her dad, and about her shop. She'd been so comfortable – and mildly tipsy – that she'd almost told him about other things too. Things she never ever felt happy discussing with anyone, because it simply hurt too much.

Still, the whole evening was turning out to be a lot nicer than she'd possibly imagined – it was a rare novelty to have adult company in the evening. It made her realise how lonely she'd been getting; the way her changing circumstances had been creeping up on her, almost without her noticing. Ellen was studying at Godwin College – medicine, which was a horrifying thought for any future patients – and although she lived at home to save money, spent most of her nights with her friends or with Jacob.

Sian had three young kids of her own; and her dad Paddy was enjoying his second childhood with an entirely new group of friends – active grey panthers who seemed to be forever booking booze cruises and taking trips to strange places.

Most nights Maggie spent working, watching TV, reading. It was nice. It was pleasant. It was safe. But it was also, she knew, a little bit sad – she was only 34, for God's sake. Other women were in the prime of their lives, and she was acting like an old maid in a Jane Austen novel. She'd be learning to play the bloody spinet and embroidering a home-sweet-home sign before she knew it. Counting grey hairs and collecting cats and waiting to die – it was an exciting future, and a ridiculous one to accept.

It had taken spending this one night in the comfort of her own home – in the company of one funny, intelligent, articulate man – to make her realise that just possibly, she was missing out.

Marco was telling her a story about Rob getting so drunk, he was arrested and locked in a jail cell wearing lederhosen and a pair of bunny ears, when they both heard the front door slam. There were a few choice swear words, and then a couple of loud thuds.

Marco paused in his tale, and looked at her with his eyebrows raised questioningly.

"That," Maggie said, "will be Ellen. She'll be drunk, and she'll have just kicked off her boots. Now she'll stagger through to the kitchen for some water, and then come in and torment us. Strap yourself in – or, you know, just pretend to be asleep. I wouldn't blame you."

They both listened, Marco grinning as he heard unsteady foot-steps do exactly what Maggie had predicted – head down the corridor to the kitchen. The sound of the fridge door opening and getting slammed shut. A few more swear words. Then, finally, the door to the living room bursting wide open, flooding the room in light from the hallway.

"Hi mummy, I'm home!", said Ellen, looming in the doorframe in shadow. "Bloody hell – what are you two up to? Why are you sitting in the dark? Do you want me to leave you alone?"

Maggie leaned over and flicked on one of the lamps. She'd not even noticed how dark it was until then, and her eyes blinked in the sudden glow.

Ellen took in the discarded beer bottles, and the pizza box, and walked fully into the room, picking up the one slice of pepperoni that was left.

"Excellent," she said to Maggie, plonking herself down on the arm of the recliner. "I see you're caring for our patient in the best possible way."

Ellen looked over at Marco, thoughtfully chewing on a mouthful of pizza as she assessed him.

"I'm Ellen," she said, between swallows.

"I'm Marco," he replied. "Nice to meet you at last. I've heard a lot about you."

"Ha!" she spluttered, almost choking. "I bet it was all bad! You look all right, Marco, considering you've just come out of hospital – though not as good as you did when—"

Maggie sharply elbowed her in the side, almost toppling her off her perch. She stared her daughter full on, and sent her a silent, pleading message: please, please don't mention the park. Don't mention the fact that we've seen him before. And whatever you do, please don't mention the way I suggested he could eat me even if I was a bit past my best-before date.

Ellen stared back at her, a slow smile creeping onto her face.

"Not as good as you probably did before mother knocked you off your bike," she finished. Maggie was so relieved to have escaped that especially embarrassing hurdle that she let the incorrect version of bike crash events slip.

"Actually, it was all my fault," Marco said, obviously amused at the banter. "I was cycling too fast, on the wrong side of the road. And I was listening to Aerosmith at the time."

"Uggh," replied Ellen, shaking her head in mock horror. "And were you wearing that?" she added, pointing to the elf-patterned jumper lying over the arm of the chair.

Marco nodded, and pulled a face. He replied: "Yeah. My sister-in-law Leah bought me a whole set. She thinks they're hilarious, and my nephew Luca does too, so I don't have much choice but to wear them."

"Well, bearing in mind your wardrobe and your taste in music, a bike crash was probably the least of your worries. So what have you two been doing all night?"

"Just talking," both Marco and Maggie said at exactly the same time, a little too quickly. Ellen narrowed her eyes and looked from one to the other, suspiciously.

"Hmm...if you say so. Any beers left, mum?"

"I'm not sure you need any more beers, love. What's that stain on your jeans?"

"It's exactly what you think it is. I must have had a dodgy pint. I did use a carrier bag, but it had those little holes in it that stop toddlers suffocating or something. So annoying – don't you think, Marco?"

"Hey, we've all been there," he said, laughter in his voice. "If in doubt, double bag, is my advice."

"It's probably good advice in all kinds of circumstances. Anyway. You're right – I don't need any more. I'll go off up to bed in a minute – I just wanted to call in and meet you, Marco, and also mum, to tell you something."

"What's that?" Maggie asked, feeling a ridiculous and momentary panic: was she pregnant? Was history going to repeat itself?

"No, don't worry, I'm not pregnant," said Ellen, wiping her now-greasy hands on her already traumatised jeans. "It's about Christmas. Jacob and his family are going to their place in Paris for the holidays, and they've invited me and a few of the others to come along. Is that all right with you? I mean, you'll have Granddad round anyway, won't you?"

Maggie kept her face bland while she processed the news. Not pregnant = good. Her daughter's first Christmas away from home = not so simple. Her first instinct was to say no. To refuse. To tell her she was too young. That she hadn't known Jacob or his family for anywhere near long enough. But the reality was different...Ellen would be 19 in a few months' time. She was already independent, strong-minded. More grown-up now than Maggie had been when she gave birth to her. And Christmas in Paris with her friends? How could she possibly compete with that – she didn't even have the first edition to give her any more. And more to the point, how could she deny her that experience? How selfish would that be?

Not trusting herself to say anything more, and conscious of the fact that this particular mini-drama was playing out in front of a man she was supposed to be caring for, she gave Ellen a quick smile and simply said: "I'm sure we can sort something out. Let's talk about it properly tomorrow, when both you and your jeans are a bit less tired and emotional."

"'Kay," said Ellen, standing up and stretching herself out. "Sounds like a plan. Goodnight you two. Don't do anything I wouldn't do."

Chapter 11

When Maggie woke up the next morning, she was greeted by a mild hangover, and the sounds of warfare wafting up from downstairs.

Guns firing, bombs exploding, and men shouting. Combining that with the dull thud behind her eyes was very confusing and made her want to hibernate. Groaning, she reluctantly pulled the duvet down from over her head, and poked one hand up into the air. It wasn't freezing cold – which meant it was past the time she usually got up, as the heating had clicked on.

She climbed out of bed, glanced at the clock on the bedside cabinet, and saw that it was almost 10am. Shit. She had to check on Marco, take some paracetamol, make sure Ellen was still alive, and get to the shop for 11 for Isabel's final fitting.

She struggled into her work 'uniform' – jeans and a T-shirt – and popped into the bathroom to brush her teeth. As she fiddled with the tube and squirted it onto the brush, she looked up and saw a yellow post-it note stuck to the mirror.

"I'm still alive!" it said, in Ellen's messy pre-doctor scrawl. Hah. She knows me too well, thought Maggie. Or maybe I'm just an extremely predictable person.

She ripped the note off, screwed it up, and tossed it into the over-flowing rubbish bin. Housework was neither her nor Ellen's speciality.

Looking into the mirror, she decided to whack on a bit of tinted moisturiser. Maybe a touch of blusher. Perhaps some mascara? No, that was too much. She was being silly. She hadn't worn make-up in the day for...well, years. Unless she had a wedding to go to, anyway. What was different about this day?

Obviously, she knew exactly what was different about this day, and couldn't bring herself to meet her reflection in the glass. She was embarrassed by her own feelings, and scurried around looking for a bobble to try and distract herself. Considering that two women with long hair used this bath room, there never seemed to be a bloody bobble lying around...she finally found one, and scooped her hair up into a pony. She didn't bother with a hair-brush – it'd only get stuck in the tangled mass. She needed a conditioning treatment. Or a wig. Or a valium.

She pulled the pony tight, then sat on the closed toilet lid and forced herself to take a deep breath and calm down.

It was just a day like any other, she told herself. It doesn't matter what you look like. It doesn't matter that there's a man downstairs. A man you like, and who you don't find physically repulsive. It doesn't matter, and you're being pathetic.

She decided she'd stop being pathetic right after she spritzed on a quick squirt of perfume. Maybe it'd make up for the fact that she didn't have time for a shower.

As she trotted barefoot down the stairs, the sounds of warfare started to be accompanied by the sounds of laughter. Whatever was going on in there, someone was enjoying it.

She pushed open the living room door, and saw Marco, sitting upright in his bed, hunched over an X Box controller, frantically twiddling buttons. Ellen was cross-legged on the recliner, pointing at the screen and screeching with laughter. Ellen. Who wanted to go away for Christmas. Well, Maggie decided, that was one to deal with later in the day.

"You are totally crap at this!" her daughter was yelling. "You've just shot your own man in the head! If there's a zombie apocalypse while you're here, Marco, you better just hide under your bed while I kick their arses for you!"

"I just need more practice, then I'll kick *your* ass!" he replied, throwing the controller down onto his lap in mock disgust and laughing.

Maggie walked properly into the room, noticing that the pizza box and beer bottles had been cleared away.

"Ah. Nothing like a bit of Call of Duty to wake you up on a winter's morning," she said, walking over to Marco's table and checking his tablet box. The pills for today had been taken, which meant she could at least avoid one battle.

"Hey," he said, smiling up at her. "How are you?"

"Fine," she replied, her eyes narrowing as she noticed that his hair was damp, and he was wearing different clothes than the ones he'd gone to bed in. A close-fitting khaki green T-shirt that moulded over his bulk, and made him look not unlike the military figures on screen.

"Did you manage to get changed all right? I could have helped."

Even as she said it, she was glad she hadn't needed to. It probably wouldn't be good for her blood pressure to see Marco without his clothes on. She might swoon, which would be embarrassing all round.

"He didn't need your help, Mum," said Ellen, switching the TV off and sauntering towards the door. She was still wearing pyjamas that had 'give me coffee or die' emblazoned on the front, and her hair was starting to be colonised by auburn dreadlocks. "He had Nanny McPhee for that. It was fun times all round while you were snoozing away. Right, gonna get a shower and turn myself into a human being...Granddad called, said he's coming round for tea. He'll bring the food."

Maggie turned back to Marco, who was swinging his legs round to the side of the bed and using the controller to lower it. He grimaced slightly as he moved, and she knew he must still be in a lot of pain.

"Nanny McPhee?" she asked, now even more confused.

"Yeah. Or Doris, as she's actually called. Leah was true to her word – she managed to find the oldest nurse in Britain to come and help me out in the mornings. So I'm clean, changed, and ready to rock – just help me into the wheelchair, will you?"

Maggie moved to his side, and Marco slung one arm around her shoulder. She made sure he had a tight grip, and when he was ready, helped him hop the two steps into the chair. He landed safely and with a slight wheeze of effort that he immediately tried to hide.

"It's okay," she said, crouching down in front of him to adjust the footrests. "I know it hurts. You don't have to pretend to be Superman for my benefit."

"But what if I *want* to pretend?" he replied, grinning at her. "What if I need to try and get my macho back after Nanny McPhee emasculated me with her evil sponge bath techniques? Can't you at least pretend to be impressed by my manly toughness?"

She glanced up at him, still kneeling down on the floor, and met his eyes. He was joking. Mainly – but there was something real there, in his expression. Something that told her it wasn't all a joke.

She gave his plaster cast a gentle pat, and stood up straight.

"I tell you what – if you survive a morning in a wedding dress shop with me, I'll be impressed. There'll be bows and veils and satin and silk and you'll have to make tea for me all morning. There might even be crying women on the premises. Is your manly toughness up to coping with all that? Your alternative is staying home getting humiliated in virtual battle by a teenaged girl."

"Wow," said Marco, grimacing. "That is a truly awesome set of options. Could I possibly just wheel myself off a cliff instead?"

"There are no cliffs near here, I'm afraid, or I'd be happy to oblige. I'll get your coat. We can call at the bakery on the way and get coffee and croissants – assuming that's not too girly for you?"

"Nah. Carbs and caffeine. That's pure man-cave stuff. Can I bring my laptop? I have the lecture at the Law Institute to prepare for. I might get some extra sympathy points now I'm a cycling war veteran, but I still need to do some more work on it. And make the arrangements for getting there."

"That's all sorted," said Maggie, walking into the hallway and grabbing his jacket. It was dark blue and super-padded, which was a good thing as the snow had settled overnight. She took hold of one of his arms – nice – and started to slip it into the sleeve as she spoke.

"I've got the Marco Mobile outside," she said as she worked, "and Rob's already explained you'll need lift access and a ramp up onto the stage and...stop wriggling! I'm just trying to help!"

"I can put my own coat on, thanks," he snapped, "I have a broken leg, my arms are working just fine! Go and get some socks on, woman – leave me alone!"

Maggie backed up, leaving him to work the zipper. He was looking flustered and annoyed, and he did have a point – barefoot in the snow sounded pretty, but would probably result in the surgical removal of all her toes. She nodded, left him alone with his grouch, and ran up the stairs.

As he heard her footsteps padding upwards, Marco sighed out one big, long, frustrated breath. He pulled the zipper up, and shook his head in annoyance. He'd come close to losing his temper again then – and it wasn't even close to being her fault.

But he was sitting there, feeling like a big fat useless baby, while she tried to manoeuvre him into his jacket – which had involved her leaning so close into him that her chest was thrust into his face. Seriously, one slight move forward, and he'd have been able to bury his head in her breasts.

She was reaching behind, stretching the jacket over his shoulders, completely unaware of the fact that she was jiggling around in front of him, crippling him with the kind of feelings that were only ever going to result in some major league embarrassment all round. His leg wasn't working – but other parts of him definitely were, and that wasn't something he wanted to confront her with first thing in the morning. Certainly not before she had her coffee.

He could hear her moving around upstairs, and knew he only had a few moments to calm himself down. He brought back to mind the arrival of Nanny McPhee, complete with warts and sensible shoes, in an attempt to calm the savage beast. Sometimes it really sucked being a man – it was like his body came with two brains, and only one of them responded to reason. The other responds to having a pretty woman thrust her curvy bits at him.

He'd slept well, soothed by beer, painkillers, and the far more pleasant than anticipated night he'd spent talking with Maggie. He'd known he found her attractive – but hadn't expected to like her as well. It made his body's reaction to her booby trap even more embarrassing. She was kind, and gentle, and good – the last thing he wanted to do was make her feel uncomfortable. Marco had the feeling that Maggie didn't even see herself as a sexual being, as a desirable woman – she'd spent so much of her adulthood as a mother, she'd missed out on the usual one-night stands and dates and flirting that other women experienced. That type of confidence was missing in her – and he'd really prefer not to physically poke her in the eye with evidence that she was wrong.

By the time she came back into the room, suited and booted and wrapped up in a woolly hat and gloves, he was feeling more in control. But just to be on the safe side, he'd leaned over and grabbed up his laptop bag, placing it on his knees and keeping a tight hold.

"Ready?" she said, her eyes flicking over him to check he was okay. "No...wait. You'll be too cold. Let me get you a scarf."

She dashed back out into the hallway, and returned with the kind of crazy patchwork-knit affair that he'd seen in re-runs of old Doctor Who episodes. She leaned down, obviously planning to wrap it around his neck for him, but he gently took hold of both her hands.

"It's all right, Maggie," he said softly, not wanting to freak out again. "I can do it. Thanks."

She simply nodded, gave him a little smile, and said "Tally ho!" as she wheeled the chair down the hallway - out into the brilliant sunlight, and a whole new day.

Chapter 12

Marco was used to snow – he lived in Chicago, where they seemed to live under feet of it every winter – but it rarely looked so pretty as it did here in Jericho. Just outside the city centre, it wasn't as grand as the Oxford colleges and libraries, but still gorgeous. To his American eyes, everything seemed magical – like a scene from Harry Potter, with the Victorian terraces and quaint boutiques and tree-lined streets. Especially when it was coated in snow, and especially when it came with a running commentary from Maggie – pointing out the best local cafes; the best deli; the little school that Ellen used to go to; the passageway that led up to St Giles and the pub where Tolkien used to call into when he was writing Lord of the Rings...it was all amazing.

He just wished he could climb out of the chair, and explore it himself. He'd been here for a week already when the accident happened – he'd used the lecture as a reason to take an extended vacation, to catch up with Luca, and to be here for the Christening – but he'd never really seen the place through a local's eyes.

Maggie brought everything to life for him, chattering away as she pushed him along in the snow, huffing and puffing slightly as she negotiated kerbs, until they reached her shop. She pulled her gloves off, and fished around in her pockets for the keys.

"Are you okay?" she asked, standing back and surveying him. His cheeks were rosier than normal thanks to the icy breeze, and there were snowflakes caught on his eyelashes, but other than that she thought he looked all right. Better than all right, in fact. "I'm sorry – I've not shut up, have I? You could have been screaming for help and I was waffling on about the lady over the road who makes her own chocolates!"

Marco reached up, took hold of one of her now-shaking hands in both of his, and gave them a gentle squeeze.

"I'm 100% great. I like you 'waffling on'. Now, let's get inside, so I can start my new job as your unpaid tea boy…weird, isn't it? When I called in here that time, we'd never seen each other before. And now you get to tuck me in at night!"

Maggie felt her face do a predictable meltdown. The curse of the ginger strikes again, she thought. Because that hadn't been the first time she'd seen him, and somehow that very small, innocent fact made her blush every time it popped into her mind.

"Yeah," she said. "Weird."

Abruptly, she turned away, and unlocked the door, pushing it open with a jingle and flicking the lights on. She wheeled Marco in, and looked on as he glanced around. It was exactly as she'd left it the day before – clean but messy, uber-feminine, and still smelling of the roses that Leah had brought her. The sewing machine was still on a table in the corner; the Christmas tree was still draped with the decorations the pixies had made, and the floor was still strewn with thread and scraps. It was ever thus.

The only difference this time was that it felt smaller – mainly because of the large man she'd brought with her.

She bit her lip sharply, and started to take off her coat and hat. Marco struggled out of his, and she left him to it, taking it from him and hanging it up on the pegs in the kitchen. She propped open the door to the room in the back, and pointed through to it.

"Everything you'll need is through there, when you feel the need for tea. It's all at waist level, and there should be enough room for you to get in and out. The loo's back there as well, so just tell me if you need help – I know you don't want to, but believe me it'll be far less macho if you end up falling, and I have to try and heave you back into that chair with your pants round your ankles. I'll nip out for the croissants and coffee in a bit...you can set yourself up with the laptop over in the corner there – I'll just get rid of those magazines – and...poo, actually I need to get a dress ready...Isabel will be here soon..."

"Isabel? Is she the bride to be?" asked Marco, experimentally pushing his wheels backwards and forwards, wondering how long it would take before he could do it entirely by himself.

"She is. And this one is...special. Well, they all are, but Isabel and her fiancé particularly. Michael has leukaemia. He's in remission, but he's still not well. Not back to normal. They have to go back and forward for blood tests all the time, and it's so not fair. They're the nicest couple you'll ever meet."

"Jeez. How old is this guy?" asked Marco.

"Only 32. It's bonkers, isn't it? They found out just after they'd set the date, and he went straight into treatment. They held on to the wedding though – I don't know, it's like it gave them something to aim for. Something to give them hope."

As she disappeared off into another room at the back, Marco reflected on the story – and promised himself he'd remember it whenever he felt he was heading back towards self-pity city. There were far worse fates than being stranded in a beautiful city with a beautiful woman and a broken leg. There was nothing wrong with him that time and some pretty strong painkillers wouldn't mend. He needed to remind himself of that when he was turning into a hobbling Christmas Grinch – or when Nanny McPhee returned with her Sponge of Evil.

He wheeled himself over to the table, and piled the wedding magazines into a corner. Yikes. Even touching them made him feel less of a man, with all their glossy covers and flowery text and picture-perfect brides smiling up at him with dazzling teeth.

Pulling the laptop up and out of the bag, he noticed two people approaching the shop front. They paused – the man tall and thin, the woman petite and blonde – and hugged each other before they came in.

Still laughing at some private joke, they stopped dead when they saw him sitting there, looking up at them. The woman frowned, and the man stood protectively in front of her, even though he was using a cane and looked like two strong puffs of wind could blow him over.

"Hi," said Marco quickly, "you must be Isabel and Michael? I'm Marco – it's nice to meet you."

He held out his hand – keen to reassure them that Maggie's shop wasn't being burgled by an invalid with a bridal magazine fetish – and smiled as the man walked over to shake it.

"Long story short, Maggie's looking after me while I get back on my feet. Literally," he said, gesturing down to his plastered leg.

Isabel closed the gap between them and shook his hand as well, looking down at the leg and grimacing in sympathy.

"Oooh. Nasty. Did you need plates?"

"No, thank God. Hopefully I'll be up and around in a few weeks...well, they say months, but I have other plans."

"I bet you do! You show 'em who's boss, Marco!" said Michael, laughing as he lowered himself tentatively into the chair opposite him. He looked about 20 years older than he should, his face thin and gaunt, his hands trembling as he placed his fingers on the table top. Marco noticed that Isabel was sneaking peeks at her fiancé, doing that thing Maggie kept doing to him – as though she could assess his vital signs just by looking. Maybe these women had secret X-ray vision or something.

On cue, Maggie bustled back into the shop front, dashing over to give both Isabel and Michael huge hugs. Her face had lit right up when she saw them, and he felt a flood of affection flow through him. She was so genuine. So full of humanity. So completely different from the women he usually dated. It kind of made him realise how shallow his own life was – something his mother had been nagging him about for years now.

Mrs Cavelli used to focus on Rob, but as he was now married, blissfully happy, and dutifully popping out heirs to the throne, she'd turned her beady eyes onto her second twin. The one who'd never brought home a serious girlfriend, never mind come close to marrying one. Eden had been the nearest he'd ever had to a proper relationship – he'd been in his late 20s, she'd been great, and maybe things would have developed in that direction given enough time. But after his father had died, everything changed. His priority had been his mother, and the family business. Everything else had taken a back seat.

Since then, nothing. Friends, sure, and a lot of fun, a lot of work. But nothing more serious. Marco didn't know why. He'd not actively avoided it. He didn't have some set-in-stone agenda to become an aging playboy. He'd simply never met anyone who affected him that much – and the aftermath of Rob's first wife, Meredith, dying, had crushed any latent desire he had to settle down. The flip side of loving someone that much was hurting that much – and seeing Rob go through years of pain and trauma had pretty much convinced Marco that that path wasn't for him. Even the happy ending Rob now had wasn't quite enough to erase the torture of those lost years – of wondering if every time he saw his brother might be the last.

It had taken time – and Leah – to bring Rob back to the land of the living. And until that miracle happened, Marco knew with hindsight, both himself and his mom had put their own lives on hold, waiting and hoping and watching as Rob self-destructed. He'd been like a time bomb – and had unintentionally sucked everyone else into the downward spiral with him.

Now, looking at Isabel and Michael, the way they so obviously adored each other, looking at Maggie and thinking of her relationship with her daughter, he was starting to wonder if he might just be missing out on something. If the golden apple could be worth reaching for after all.

Or maybe, he thought, shaking his head to clear away the thoughts, I'm just on too many damn drugs...

Chapter 13

"So," said Maggie's dad, a plate of Chinese noodles on his lap. "How are you liking it here so far, Marco?"

Paddy O'Donnell was in his 60s, and bore a close resemblance to Father Christmas. His beard was full, bushy and white, and his belly heaped over his belted trousers in a celebration of all things beer. His eyes – a sharp, probing blue – were crinkled in the folds of his face, and currently giving Marco a thorough fatherly once-over.

Marco himself was standing next to his bed, practising staying upright with the use of his crutches. Maggie was looking on, one eye on her food, the other on her patient. Maybe she was worried that if he toppled over, he'd land on the huge Christmas tree, taking it down like a Yeti coated in tinsel.

"It's as good as it can be under the circumstances, Mr O'Donnell," Marco replied, starting to feel the strain on his right leg and wondering how long he could manage. "Your daughter is a saint for putting up with me."

"Call me Paddy, son," he replied. "And she is that – don't know if she told you, but I went right off the rails for a while a few years back. Booze. Black-outs. Loose women."

"Dad!" squealed Maggie, outraged. "There are some things nobody needs to hear about! Keep your loose women stories to yourself, for goodness' sake!"

"Anyway," he continued, grinning at her response. "She was the one that pulled me out of it eventually. Don't know how she coped – her mum going, the baby arriving, me toddling off down the road to nowhere..."

"I don't think I exactly helped the situation by getting pregnant, Dad," said Maggie, her voice quiet and soft. Still, after all these years, so conscious of the upheaval her one night of drunken fun had caused. Even after all the joy that Ellen had brought them, she still shuddered when she remembered sitting in the family bath room, crying over the three pregnancy test sticks that all stubbornly refused to be negative. Shocked and sobbing, and wishing more than anything that her mum was there to talk to.

"Well, it didn't seem like good news at the time, did it?" said Paddy, putting his plate down. "But she was a blessing in disguise, that child. And you've done a great job raising her, love. Where is she anyway? Out larking, is she? I see there's a new addition to the tree this year..."

Every Christmas, Ellen contributed her own fresh take on the festive season. It had started when she was little, with angels made out of cardboard and tin foil; graduated to Santas constructed from toilet roll tubes, and as the years progressed – and Ellen's sense of humour progressed with them – delved into the more Tim Burton-esque reaches of the Christmas landscape. There was the vampire angel from her Twilight phase; and a collection of papier mâché zombie elves from the Walking Dead era. Last year there'd been a hand-drawn card of the Godwin College crest decorated with glitter, to mark the fact that she'd been accepted at university.

So, thought Maggie, turning to inspect it – what potential monstrosity awaited them this time? She peered at the tree, and saw it straight away. Perched precariously in the branches of bushy pine was an old Action Man figure, in army fatigues, wielding a miniature plastic rifle. One of its legs was coated in what looked like toilet paper, and he was wearing a tiny pipe cleaner crown.

"Ha!" exclaimed Maggie, grinning up at Marco. "You're honoured – you'll be forever remembered at O'Donnell family Christmases from now on!"

Marco was smiling too, although she could see a clammy sweat had broken out on his forehead. She fought the urge to sweep back his dark hair and check his temperature; she was getting a pretty good idea by now of how important it was for Marco to at least try and appear independent. He wouldn't appreciate a mothering intervention when he was doing his very best to stay upright.

"Hey, I feel privileged," he said, leaning almost imperceptibly back a few inches further onto the side of the bed. "I need to get a photo of that for posterity. I might use it for my business cards – I think she's caught the real me."

Maggie smiled in response, then stood up, collected plates of leftovers, and hurriedly deposited them in the kitchen. He needed to lie down, to rest, to stop pushing himself – but she had the feeling he wouldn't give in while she was in the room.

Sure enough, by the time she returned, he'd clambered back onto the bed, and was sprawled across the top of the covers. He had his arms crossed behind his head, and all kinds of impressive stuff was going on in the bicep region. It shouldn't have been possible for a man to look both exhausted and macho, but somehow he pulled it off.

"Anyway, love," said Paddy, registering the way she looked at Marco and tucking it away to think about later, "I wanted to talk to you about Christmas. I know we usually all spend it together, but Jim's been offered a last minute cabin on a cruise to the Canaries. Half price cancellation. Sunshine, company, and as much booze as you can shake a stick at. He's got nobody else to go with him, and I must admit I'm tempted."

Maggie had come to a standstill in the doorway, her eyes on Marco but her ears taking in what her father was saying. Processing the words. Eventually coming to the correct conclusion: another rat was deserting her fast sinking Christmas ship.

"Right. Yes. It sounds lovely, Dad," she said, trying to hide the sinking sense of disappointment she could feel creeping over her.

"You don't mind do you, love? I mean, Ellen will be here, won't she?"

Maggie simply nodded, walking over to the Christmas tree and busying herself with collecting stray stands of lametta from the floor around it. She clenched her eyes tight together, willing the tears that were brewing there to stay away, until she felt composed enough to turn around, with a smile as bright and as false as the lametta.

"Of course I don't mind, Dad," she replied. "You and Jim have fun. I'll ping off an email to the British Embassy putting them on high alert later."

Paddy snorted with laughter, and got up to go. He brushed his trousers down, and gave Maggie a quick kiss before leaving. He had a 'hot date with a pint of Guinness and a darts board', apparently. Maggie watched her dad plodding carefully through the snow down the path, taking a right hand turn towards their local, shivering in the moonlight as she closed the door behind him. She walked slowly back into the living room, and silently headed to the curtains. She paused before she drew them together, looking out at the houses across the street. Like hers, they were lit up with gaudy Christmas lights; dazzling trees peeking out from the bay windows, wreaths glistening in the frost on front doors. The garden directly opposite was festooned with neon baubles and a giant inflatable Santa that glowed in the dark, along with reindeers made out of shining orange bulbs.

She'd always loved Christmas. She was a terrible cook – there was a reason everyone who visited her brought food with them

– but always made an effort on Christmas Day. They'd had dried out turkey; burned sprouts, and potatoes roasted to within an inch of their spuddy lives. But at least they'd always had them together – her, Ellen, and Dad. A small but perfectly formed family unit.

Now, for the first time ever, she'd be alone. Alone with the giant Christmas tree and a bottle of Baileys and, if she was sensible about it, a Marks and Sparks microwave dinner for one. She felt drained, empty, sad. The very opposite of all the festivity around her.

"Why didn't you tell him?" said Marco, his voice quiet and serious. Christ, thought Maggie, jumping – she'd completely forgotten he was there. She'd walked straight past him on the bed, over to the window, lost in her own pathetically melancholy thoughts. She wouldn't last a day at nursing school: 'Oh, I'm sorry Mr Smith, I didn't notice you screaming in agony, I'd broken a nail.'

"Tell him what?" she asked, crossing her arms over her chest defensively, gathering in warmth.

"About Ellen. About her going to Paris. About the fact that you'll be on your own for Christmas."

"Oh...that. Well, it doesn't matter, does it? I'm a big girl. It's fine...absolutely fine."

She decided she needed a drink. A big one. With bells on it. It had been a lovely day, seeing Isabel and Michael and sharing in their happiness. Knowing her dress was perfect; knowing that all the Christmas dresses were perfect. Having Marco to keep her amused in the shop. Eating cranberry muffins for lunch. A text from Ellen saying she was heading to the Ann Summers store to get her Christmas present (hopefully a joke). Her dad turning up with two big bags full of food from her favourite takeaway. She'd felt warm and busy and lucky to have such a full life – she'd even managed to avoid thinking too hard about the Paris issue.

And now, she just felt deflated – and annoyed with herself for being so selfish. The two people she loved most in the world had the chance to enjoy pretty spectacular Christmases – she should be happy for them, not miserable for herself.

"I'm getting a drink," she said, walking towards the door. "Do you want one?"

As she walked past the bed, Marco's hand shot out, grabbing hold of her arm. She tried instinctively to pull away, but his grip held fast – his leg might be broken but there was nothing wrong with his upper body strength.

"You're hurting me," she said quietly, fixing him with what she hoped was a stern stare.

"I'm sorry about that, but I want to talk to you. If you leave this room, I'll try and chase you – and if I fall over and break my other leg, it'll all be your fault."

Maggie looked down at the big hand wrapped around her arm. Looked at the handsome man who owned it, his face serious as she'd ever seen it.

"Okay," she said. "I wouldn't want that to happen. Leah would never forgive me. What do you want to talk about?"

When Marco realised she was staying, he loosened his grip, let his hand trail down her arm until it found her fingers. Wrapped his in hers just in case she decided to make a run for it. Her hand was soft and pliant in his; her skin still cool to the touch. She looked defeated, and gloomy, and just a little bit scared. He'd seen sides of Maggie he didn't expect since he'd been here – her warmth, humour, and occasionally sparks of fire. But now she'd retreated into herself, and looked like she'd rather be anywhere else in the world than standing there, next to him.

"Get in," he said, scooting over to one side of the bed, and giving her hand a tug. "There's plenty of room."

She tried to break free, but he held on to her hand, pulling her closer until she was slammed right up against the edge of the bed.

"What?! No! Don't be daft!" she said, her voice shrill, eyes rolling slightly like a panicked horse.

"Get in! I think you need a hug, and I happen to have a black belt in hugging. Don't worry – your virtue's safe with me, I don't really think I'm up to anything more."

Even as he said it, he hoped it was true. That his body wouldn't betray him; that they wouldn't have an 'is that a plaster cast or are you just pleased to see me?' moment.

"Come on. You know you want to," he said, letting go of her hand and patting the space next to him.

Maggie couldn't help but smile at his tone. Against the odds, he could still make her laugh, even when she felt – temporarily, she was sure – that her world was falling apart. And maybe he was right...maybe she did need a hug. They'd been in pretty short supply for a long time now – Ellen was too old and too cool; her dad was always busy, and the brides she coached through their wedding angst were inevitably trembling and terrified when she hugged them. Sometimes a little bit teary and snotty as well. Maybe it would be nice, just for a minute, to let go – to feel like someone bigger and stronger than her could take over for five blissful minutes.

Anyway, she thought, gazing at Marco, and the spot he was gesturing to right next to him – what was the worst thing that could happen? Deciding not to answer that, she kicked off her ballet pumps and sat down on the edge of the bed.

He immediately pulled her down towards him, scooping her up into his arms so her face was resting on his chest. Her head was snuggled beneath his chin, and she curled up into his body, glad the broken leg was on the other side. She could hear his heart thudding strongly away, and tentatively threw one arm around his waist. He smelled of soap and shampoo and some kind of delicious man fragrance that she presumed was all his. And he felt...

good. God, he felt so good. Those brawny arms wrapped around her; that solid chest beneath her cheek; the firm line of his jaw resting on top of her hair.

Her hand came into contact with bare flesh where his T-shirt had ridden up, and she bit her lip to stop herself letting it drift upwards, allowing her fingers to search out more of that silky skin and powerful muscle. She tasted blood in her mouth, and realised she'd bitten a little too hard.

She settled for a moment, and they both stayed silent. God only knew what he was thinking – that she needed a long session with a hairbrush, probably.

"So," he eventually said, giving her a gentle squeeze, "what gives? Why didn't you tell your dad about Ellen – he'll find out eventually, and then they'll both feel bad."

"I know," she replied, glad she didn't have to look him in the eyes while they had this conversation. "That's exactly why I didn't tell him. I don't want either of them to feel bad – I want them both to have a great Christmas. I have a master plan...something that involves a made-up trip, or a last minute invitation to spend December 25th with Gerard Butler. Something I can tell them both to avoid them feeling sad for me. I don't want anybody pitying me – which I'm sure you can understand, Mr Macho Pants."

He snorted with laughter, and Maggie felt his fingers in her hair, playing and stroking and gently tugging in a way that made her even more conscious of the fact that he wasn't just a patient. That he wasn't just an amusing house guest. That he was the first man she'd fancied – to use the technical term – for many, many years.

"I get that, I do. My pants are indeed macho – it's an Italian thing, genetically programmed, I can't help it. But there's a difference between being pitied and being loved – and Ellen and Paddy? They love you."

"I know. I really do. And maybe I'm being a knob – I've just been caught out by it all. We've had Christmas together every year since Ellen was born. Her dad emigrated to New Zealand with his family when she was one – she's been out there to see him, there are no hard feelings, he's got another couple of kids now. But Christmas has always been…well, ours. It's special, you know?"

"I know. I understand. It's an emotional time of year. Rob used to hibernate in Scotland for weeks beforehand, hiding away from all of us – it was the anniversary of Meredith's death, and he couldn't stand the pity either. It was never the same for me and my mom, back in Chicago, knowing he was over here suffering. And we'd have done anything to help him – just like Ellen and Paddy would do anything for you. If you only asked."

Maggie considered what he'd said, while at the same time luxuriating in the feel of those long, strong fingers sweeping through her hair, casually caressing the nape of her neck, the side of her face. Black belt in hugs and then some.

Without noticing it, one of her legs had crept over him, draped across his stomach, so she was resting against the firm outline of his body. It should have felt weird. Instead, it felt delicious – and strangely natural. This was the closest she'd been to a man for as long as she could remember, but somehow it still felt safe. Comfortable. And arousing. She found herself wondering how all this would feel if they were naked. If Marco didn't have that T-shirt on – if his chest was bare, his skin against her skin, her hand allowed to roam and explore and tease…he shifted slightly, inching away from her fractionally, and she wondered if she'd hurt him.

"You okay down there?" he asked. "Have you fallen asleep?"

"Um…no…sorry. Just thinking."

About you, naked, she added silently. She needed to get a grip, or she was going to make a complete tit of herself, she decided. Not only would she be pitied by her family for being a sad, lonesome

Christmas has-been, but she'd have to live with the humiliation of having tried to sexually molest a poor innocent disabled man in her own home.

She sat up abruptly, perched on the edge of the bed and turned her back on him. She swept her hair into some kind of loose order, and waited a few seconds, hoping her pulse rate would go back to normal and her face would stop looking like a tomato sometime soon.

Maggie stood up, turned to face him. He was propped up, arms straining, looking at her with a perplexed expression.

"Sorry. You're right, about everything," she said. "I just need to think about it. See how it all feels tomorrow. Maybe try and be positive about it – Ellen's moving on, it's inevitable. Maybe it's time I started working on my own life, instead of focusing on hers. I need to break that habit."

"Okay," he replied, nodding. "That sounds right. And maybe I can help. How about this for a master plan? Come with me."

"Come with you where?" she asked, frowning in confusion.

"Come with me to Scotland. Leah would love to see you; I'd get a free escort – we could even take Nanny McPhee, make it an outing. You wouldn't be alone, and Ellen and Paddy would be guilt-free for Christmas. I know it's not Gerard Butler, but it could work. What do you say?"

Maggie gazed at him, taking it all in. The brawny body that she now knew a bit too well; the dark waves of hair that really needed a trim; the fierce hazel eyes. The cheekbones, the jaw, the wide, curving mouth...God, the mouth. It felt sinful to even look at it.

"Thank you, Marco," she replied. "But I have to say no."

Chapter 14

Nanny McPhee was bustling about her business when Maggie walked into the room the next morning.

The ancient nurse had him stripped down to his boxers, and he suspected that at any minute, she was going to start scrubbing behind his ears and telling him he could grow potatoes back there. At least, he thought, as he endured her efforts, it was nature's anti-dote to thinking about Maggie.

Last night, on the bed with her, had been disconcerting in every way. Once she'd given in and climbed on there with him, wrapping her curvy body into his, he'd been lost. That red hair of hers was splayed all over the place, so close he could smell her shampoo, and he'd been physically incapable of keeping his hands out of it. She fit so snugly into his arms, so perfectly, like they'd been designed as a matching pair. He'd lain like that with other women, obviously, but he'd never felt that same rush before. That crazy rush of the need to protect and comfort her combined with the need to do some far less gentlemanly things to her. Things that he probably couldn't even manage, hostage as he was to the damned plaster cast.

He'd concentrated desperately hard on the conversation, on saying what he thought needed to be said, trying to ignore the small movements she was making, the way her hand was resting on the bare skin of his belly. The fact that if she had just looked up – just tilted her head so he could look into those green eyes, see what signals she was sending – he could have kissed her. Started something that he probably couldn't have finished – at least in any great style – but he sure as hell wanted to.

When her leg had come across him, he thought he was going to have real problems. There he was, dispensing hugs and giving advice on complex family dynamics, all with a complete humdinger of a hard-on. It would have scared the living daylights out of her – and part of him had been relieved when she stood up to leave. The remnants of those urges, though, probably explained his next idiot move - asking her to come to Scotland with him.

The fact that she'd said no was surely a good thing. It was stupid to have even asked. This whole experience was starting to veer into uncharted territory, and he wasn't sure he was ready for the journey. With any other woman, he'd have been glad to go along for the mutually pleasurable ride. With this one? He wasn't so sure. He kind of...liked her too much. Which made no sense at all.

You, Marco Cavelli, he told himself, are turning into a girl. Get a grip of yourself. And don't be so arrogant – she said no anyway.

And now, with perfect timing, just as he was at his least impressive – feeling like a girl and getting hand-washed by an octogenarian – there she was. Standing in the doorframe, hair all over the place, in her usual jeans and T-shirt. There were dark circles under her eyes, which gave him the impression she'd slept about as well as he had, and she had a slightly stupefied expression on her face. She was probably blinded by Nanny McPhee's warts.

"Oh," she said, her eyes travelling over his bare chest and shoulders, then looking abruptly away. "I thought you'd finished. I'm sorry, I'll go and...do something else..."

"Almost done," said Doris, standing upright and grabbing a towel. She started to rub at Marco, drying him off with brisk and humiliating efficiency, whipping the towel across his thighs and stomach as though he wasn't even alive. Just then, he thought, as he closed his eyes and tried to think himself into a happy place, he kind of wished that he wasn't. He battled the urge to share a few choice words with Doris – that would be rude, she was just doing her job, and Maggie would hate it – and consoled himself by gripping the sheets of the bed so hard his knuckles turned white.

When she finally finished, and strolled over to get out a clean T-shirt, Marco opened his eyes again, hoping that Maggie would have disappeared in a puff of smoke. No such luck. She was still standing there, staring. And...laughing? Was she laughing at him? She had her hand held over her mouth to try and hide it, but her eyes gave her away. They were sparkling and wet and...yup, definitely laughing. Heck. At least he was good for something, he told himself.

Just when he thought it couldn't get any worse, Ellen pushed past her and right into the room. Far less restrained than her mother, she let out a mighty wolf whistle at the sight of the nearly naked man sitting there, which earned her stern glances from Nanny McPhee. Great, thought Marco – maybe they could invite the rest of the street in as well? Have a little party? Maybe film it all and put it on YouTube?

He managed to keep his mouth shut until Doris approached with the shirt, taking hold of his arms and holding them up in the air, as though he were a helpless kid who couldn't even dress himself.

"No! Thank you, I'm fine!" he said through gritted teeth, swiping the T-shirt from her hands mid-air and bunching it up on his lap. It was one humiliation too far. "All good now, Doris – thanks so much, see you soon!"

The nurse looked momentarily peeved, but started to clear up her paraphernalia and prepared to leave. Ellen was lounging around on the recliner, laughing out loud. At least Maggie had

had the decency to try and hide it, though a few giggles were escaping by now.

"Marco," said Ellen, pointing one finger at him, "don't you know there are impressionable women living in this house? I mean, you're not my type – there's just too much of you and you're old enough to be my dad – but you're playing with fire here. Mother might explode with lust, and poor Doris probably hasn't seen the like of it for years..."

"Hush your mouth," said Doris, zipping up her bag and standing up straight, "I might have a sexy toy boy waiting for me at home for all you know, duckie. Right. See you tomorrow."

Having shut them all up with that zinger, the nurse nodded her farewells and made a brisk exit – out into a still snowy but slightly less frigid Oxford. Maggie thought the snow would hold off today, maybe even start to clear. And picturesque as it was, getting around was a whole lot easier without it.

"Coffee?" she said to Marco, who was – thankfully – now covering himself up with a navy blue T-shirt. Ellen was a cheeky minx, but she'd unintentionally hit a sore nerve – the sight of all that bare flesh, on top of last night's unexpected intimacy, had led Maggie to believe that it would indeed be physically possible for her to explode with lust. Which would be messy.

Marco's head popped out of his top, hair scuffed in all directions, and he let out a desperate 'yes, please!'.

When she returned with two steaming mugs, Ellen was already grilling him.

"So, Marco, when are you leaving us?" she asked, giving her mum the evil eye for not bringing her a coffee as well.

"If all goes to plan, December 23. It's a long journey, but I'm feeling stronger every day. If the weather doesn't get any worse, Rob'll send a driver for me. If the roads are bad, I guess I'll have to fly to Aberdeen and take it from there."

"You say all this very casually, hiring drivers and catching flights. Are you lot loaded or something?" she asked, with the complete lack of inhibition that both made Maggie cringe and proud at the same time. Ellen, it had to be said, did not suffer from any crises of confidence.

"Yep," replied Marco, taking a tentative sip of coffee and remaining unperturbed by the interrogation. "Totally."

"Hmmm...that must be nice. And what are you doing here – some kind of lecture?"

"Yes again. The Law Institute holds a series of them during the vacation, invites an international audience, writes it up for journals, that kind of thing. I thought I'd spend a bit of time exploring the UK while I was here, but so far, I've mainly seen Oxford, and most of that either in the company of a two-year-old, or in the company of your mother and a broken leg. Not that I'm complaining."

Ellen took it all in, filing away the information, and then turned her piercing gaze to Maggie.

"And what about you, mum? What have you got on for the next few weeks, apart from tending to your hunky invalid, that is?"

"Gaynor, Lucy and Isabel are all getting married. You already know that."

"Hah," said Ellen, "three weddings and a lecture. Sounds like an especially boring chick flick. Well I'm hoping to head off to London on the 20th, if that's okay with you – there's a flight the next day that we can all get together for our Paris trip. *Is* that okay with you? I've not really seen you much since I mentioned it."

Maggie concentrated on the patterns the steam rising from her mug was making, and carefully avoided meeting Marco's eyes.

"Yes, of course it's okay – as long as you can arrange for me to speak to Jacob's parents beforehand. And yeah, I know, you're an adult – but that's a deal breaker."

"Are you worried in case they sell me into slavery?"

"No, I want to warn them what they're letting themselves in for. Look, I did have something planned for your present, but... well, Father Christmas kind of stuffed up the delivery on that one, so I'll get some cash together instead. You can change it into Euros and spend it all on croissants and fake moustaches. But I warn you now, if you want clothes washing, they need to be removed from the jumble sale you're holding on your bedroom floor and deposited in the basket. Otherwise I'll leave them to grow mould."

"Fair enough. Sounds like a deal. Thanks Mum – this is very cool of you, and I'll get you Jacob's mum's number. Right, I'll leave you to it, kids – I'm sure you have exciting plans for the day, and I'm off round to Rebecca's. I might stay over – I'll text you if I do. Laters!"

With a breezy wave, she left the room, abandoning Marco and Maggie to the first even vaguely awkward silence they'd had since he'd arrived.

She glanced at him through the coffee mug haze. He was wearing a half smile, and his eyebrows were raised.

"I know! Okay, I know! And I will tell them both, eventually, as soon as I've planned my solo trip to Bali, or whatever..."

"Hey," replied Marco, holding his hands up in the air, "don't shoot the messenger. It's your life, it's your kid. You play it however it feels right. I can't even shower myself – I'm in no position to tell you what to do."

"Your situation is a temporary setback," said Maggie, smiling sadly, "mine might be permanent. Anyway – thanks for being so... kind. Last night. You're supposed to be here recuperating, not consoling me."

"No problem," replied Marco. "I'm a multi-purpose pain in the ass. Now, what are your plans for today? I have the lecture in a few days, and need to get some work done on it. Can I stay here? Are you going in to the shop?"

"No, I don't need to. I have a few errands to run. I need to go and sell my body on Cornmarket, see if I can raise a few quid for Ellen's trip – but the rest of the day I can be here if you need me. I have some designs to work on."

"What was it, by the way?" he asked. "The present you'd got her? Was it anything to do with that book you were scooping up from the floor on the day we, ah, crashed into each other's lives?"

"I thought you were passed out for that bit...but yes. It is, well it was, a first edition of Alice in Wonderland, the one with the illustrations by Mabel Lucie Attwell. Now, it's a rather crumpled pile of old paper in my bedroom. But not to worry – she'll probably prefer cash anyway. The pages have dried out, I might be able to frame some of the pictures and put them up in the hallway. In all honesty, I think I was buying it as much for myself as I was for her. It's a book my mother read to me, and I read to her...but she's not at an age where terminal sentimentality has set in yet, lucky thing. Anyway. That's gloomy. Tell me about your lecture. What's it on?"

"You really want to know?" he asked, sensing that she was keener to change the subject than to hear about his work.

"Of course. You had to learn all about hemming and darts yesterday. I'm sure law is just as much fun as that."

"Okay," he said, grinning at her. "You asked for it. The lecture is called – and hold onto your sides, now, lady – 'Co-operation in international business law: the trans-Atlantic litigation hub.'"

He paused, looked at her reaction, and laughed out loud.

"Hey, Maggie – what's wrong with your eyes? They've gone all glazed..."

"No, honestly!" she chirped back, putting as much fake enthusiasm into it as she could. "It sounds great – you had me at 'litigation hub'!"

"I know. It's irresistible, right? It's pretty much written. I just need to go over some notes, check the presentation, that kind of thing. I can set myself up here, do it while you're in town prostituting yourself outside the bureau de change. What about these weddings you need to attend? When are they?"

"The first is this weekend. Gaynor – the lady with the huge dress, you met her when you came into the shop that time? Then Lucy the day after. Then next is Isabel and Michael, on Christmas Eve...I'm looking forward to that one so much; they really deserve a special day after everything they've been through."

"They sure do," said Marco nodding. "And do you always go to the weddings?"

"Not always – but I often get invited. It just happens that these three are all dresses I've made from scratch – not alterations, or dresses they've picked from stock. Ones I've made just for them. It takes a long time, a lot of contact, and by the end of it, we've often become close. Plus maybe from their perspective it's handy to have me on standby, in case of some terrible wardrobe malfunction."

"I'm sure that's not the only reason, Maggie. I saw the way you were with Isabel...it's like you've been on a journey with them. Become part of their lives. It's lovely that you get to go along."

Maggie smiled in agreement, though inside she wasn't so sure. She'd been doing this for years – starting off working with an older woman when she was just 19, learning her trade, building up enough experience and courage to eventually open her own place. She'd been to countless weddings, and every single one of them had reduced her to rubble.

She was always happy for the couple, and thrilled when everything went to plan. Professionally proud of the dresses. But...she always arrived alone, and always went home alone. Spending your whole life wrapped up in other people's romance was a sure-fire way to highlight the starkness of life as a single parent. And in more recent years, being surrounded by young children had started to have equal bite – much as she loved kids, they were also a bittersweet reminder of everything she'd lost.

But, it occurred to her, perhaps, at least for the next few events, she could do something to change that – and actually use the 'plus one' she usually declined. Not be the wallflower, and actually have someone to talk to – if not dance with.

"Maybe," said Maggie, hiding her nerves behind another gulp of coffee, "you'd like to come with me? I completely understand if you want to stay here instead, and I'll only be gone a couple of hours, but, well, if you wanted to…"

"Will there be cake?" he asked.

"Traditionally so, yes."

"And beer?"

"Pretty much always, Marco."

"And do you wear a fancy dress and gussy yourself up?"

"Ha! I do my best with what nature and the woman at the make-up counter in Boots gave me."

"Well in that case," he said, shooting her one of those slow, easy smiles that always made her feel weak at the knees and pretty much everywhere above, "count me in."

Chapter 15

"I feel like a homeless person," said Marco, gesturing down at the new black jogging pants he was wearing.

"Well you don't look like one, or luckily smell like one," replied Maggie, taking in the smart white shirt and navy tie. They'd tried suit trousers, but it was just too hard – they couldn't accommodate the cast. "Everyone will understand – they'll take one look at your leg and get it. The rest of you looks...fine."

He quirked his eyebrows up at her, and she turned away, pretending to check her handbag instead. He looked more than fine. He looked edible. She was secretly glad he hadn't been able to pull off the full suited and booted look – he would have been too much to cope with. James Bond if he'd eaten all his spinach and gained a sense of humour.

She pulled down the driver seat mirror and checked her face. Yes, she thought, it's still there. I still have a face, and predictably enough it's still blushing. And it's still as made-up as it was ever going to get with your limited skill set.

She was wearing her standard Guest At A Wedding frock – the most expensive single item of clothing she owned. A simple dark green thing, fitted, with a tasteful V-neckline. She was never much for dressing up anyway, and always believed that at other people's weddings, the focus was always quite rightly on the bride. Nobody cared much what she looked like. Normally, she wasn't that bothered either – but for some mysterious reason she couldn't quite fathom, had made an extra effort for this one.

She'd straightened her hair, which flowed down her back as far as her waist once all the curls and tangles were removed, and put in the dangling jade ear-rings her mum had bought her so many years ago. She'd accessorized with black heels, a black clutch, and a beefy American stud. It was a whole new look.

"Don't worry," said Marco, laying one hand on her knee in a way that was probably supposed to be reassuring, but simply made her pulse spike, "you're gorgeous. Your hair is...amazing."

"Yeah," replied Maggie, snapping the mirror back up into place and smiling. "I really thought that when I was 15 and my nickname was Duracell. Anyway. I'm ready if you are. And I'm bringing the chair, no matter what you say. Unless you fancy wrestling me to the ground to stop me, there's nothing you can do about it."

"Tyrant," he said, taking a deep breath as he prepared to clamber out of the passenger seat.

Gaynor's wedding was at a hotel about four miles out of the city centre. Although it was near the motorway turn-off, it was set in its own grounds, complete with a large lake, a colony of swans, and various picturesque outdoor areas designed specifically with wedding photos in mind. Maggie had been to several weddings here, and they'd all been raucous – pretty much everyone attending stayed over in the hotel, which led to all sorts of interesting behaviour. She'd never checked, but had a private theory that there was often a spike in business at the maternity ward nine months after one of these affairs.

The snow had, as she'd suspected, stopped falling afresh, and the roads had cleared into grey slush. The hotel, though, seemed to have sustained the illusion of a picture-perfect whiteout – the lawns were coated and dazzlingly white, and all of the trees lining the driveway were shining with glittering strings of Christmas lights.

The ceremony had taken place in late afternoon, and as they arrived for the evening party, the sky had faded from sunlight to a slinky silver moon. Glancing inside the building, Maggie could see the revelry in full swing, a dancefloor bustling with bodies. Gaynor herself was taking up most of the space in her huge dress, one of the younger bridesmaids holding her hands. She had, at least, settled for smaller frocks for the children – a blessing as far as Maggie was concerned. She couldn't help but smile as she looked at them – and to wonder how that trick with the toy gun had gone.

"Wait here while I get the stuff," said Maggie, opening the car door and getting carefully out. She wasn't used to heels, and the floor was still frosty.

"Aye aye captain," replied Marco, watching as she tottered around to the back. She really did look fantastic, he thought. Like one of those pre-Raphaelite paintings come to life – all shining auburn hair and luscious curves. And the shoes...shiny and black and pointy. Enough to give a man a fetish. It was yet another Maggie O'Donnell for him to marvel at – she looked like some kind of glamorous earth goddess, and didn't seem to know it at all.

He'd been haggling with the earth goddess all day about that ages-old conflict, Crutches vs Wheelchair. Marco was insisting that he was ditching the chair completely from now on, that he'd never get his strength back if he kept 'sitting his fat ass in it all the time'. Maggie had responded that his ass was far from fat, and went on to use that annoying thing called logic to point out that later in the evening, possibly after a drink or two, he might be glad of it.

She'd forced him into a compromise where they took both, and he was going along with it. He was an attorney – and he knew when logic had defeated him. He'd taken pain pills before he left, sent a photo of his down-and-out-does-wedding look to Rob and

Leah to give them a giggle, and was ready to party. Or at least spend the night surreptitiously sneaking glances at his partner for the evening. Back home, weddings were usually prime hunting sites for fun and foxy female companionship, but this woman had his brain so scrambled, he probably wouldn't notice if naked supermodels were serving up the champagne.

She appeared back by his side of the car, shivering in the frosty evening, her bare arms goosebumping so much they made him feel cold as well. She had the chair all set up, and the crutches leaned up against the side of the rear doors. Huh. They'd agreed that he'd walk in, not get wheeled, but she seemed to have changed her mind on him.

"Oh please don't argue," said Maggie as he stared at the chair she was brandishing. "Be a gent and get in. I'm freezing my tits off out here."

He laughed, and started the careful climb from his seat, lifting his broken leg out first and sliding his body round. He took hold of the frame and pulled himself up.

"Well that would be a pity," he said, lowering himself, with her guiding hands, down into the chair. She'd beaten him again – using the gentleman card against him.

"Here, hold these," she replied, giving him her clutch and a large silver gift bag to hold. He took a peek inside – and saw it was full of some kind of chocolate. It probably beat a coffee maker, he decided, as wedding presents went.

She locked the door, and pushed him towards the entrance lobby, saying she'd come back for the crutches when she had him 'all set up'.

Once inside, the noise levels hit them both like a baseball bat to the ears. The large function room was edged with chairs and tables, all decorated with purple and silver cloths and bows, and every single one seemed to be laden down with enough alcohol to fill the lake outside. Pint glasses, champagne flutes, bottled beer and wine were scattered everywhere.

A DJ was set up on the stage, and was presumably having the easiest gig of his life – this was a crowd that had come primed to party. He probably could have played a remix of the Moldovan national anthem and still had people out there attempting the Macarena.

He was currently spinning Kylie's Can't Get You Out Of My Head, and the whole dancefloor was pulsating with varying degrees of rhythm. The ages ranged from toddlers being held by their chubby hands through to an elderly couple who looked like they'd both have a framed telegram from the Queen back at home. A couple of the younger kids were doing the traditional 'slide across the floor in my best clothes' routine Maggie had seen many times before, disappearing in and out of dancing legs, pumped up on cake and excitement.

She took it all in, and grinned. Looked like a good day had been had by all, and an even better night was ahead. She momentarily regretted driving – this one was going to get messy.

Maggie pushed Marco's chair towards a partially unoccupied table, mumbled a few words to him, and disappeared back off into the night to retrieve the magical crutches. She could, of course, have left them there – stranding him in the chair. But knowing Marco, he'd find a way to get up and about, and probably not the safest way either. He'd told her stories about his life back home in the States, and a lot of them seemed to involve balls – the kind that got thrown around a football field, or bounced on a basketball court. Staying so inactive was driving him mad, she knew.

By the time she returned, he'd gained two new fans. Gaynor was standing next to him – she probably wanted to sit down, but the fantastical proportions of her frock made it a tricky move. And her niece, six-year-old Ella, was perched on Marco's lap. He was spinning the chair around in small circles as fast as he could, which was making her squeak with delight. Her bridesmaid dress was already smudged with chocolate, and her blonde curls were making a bid for freedom from the restraints of her headband.

"Go fast, go faster!" she was squealing, clinging on to his neck with her skinny little arms. He obliged, provoking more screams, and then came to a gradual stop, fake panting with the effort.

"More – do it some more!" demanded Ella, bouncing up and down in excitement. "It's like Alton Towers!"

"I can't, sweetheart," he said, smiling up at Maggie. "The boss lady is back. And I'm feeling real dizzy. And hungry – could you maybe go and fetch me some snacks?"

The little girl nodded, jumped down from his lap, and trotted off in her now-bare feet to the buffet table. She cast a sweet smile back in his direction as she went. She'd probably remember him for the rest of her life, thought Maggie. He was a natural with kids – and no matter how much he joked about his single lifestyle, he was a man born to be a father. A man who should, one day, be surrounded by Lucas and Ellens of his own.

"You do realise she'll only bring you cake, don't you?" asked Gaynor, whose face was flushed with the excitement of the day. That, and possibly several glasses of celebratory champagne.

"That's what I'm counting on," he replied, giving her an easy grin. "I'm only here for the cake."

Gaynor – newly married as she was – still looked a little bit smitten, and did a double-take when she realised Maggie was standing behind her, holding two crutches.

"Maggie!" she yelled, giving her as much of a hug as the ginorma-dress and the crutches would allow. "I'm so glad you came – and that you brought Marco with you! I recognised him from that day in the shop as soon as I saw him. He told me what happened – that he's staying with you now. That was a lucky break, eh?"

As she said it, she gave Maggie a hard nudge, making sure she got the gag.

Maggie passed the crutches to Marco to hold, and picked up the gift bag from the table.

"The jury's still out on that one – he's not the world's easiest of patients...anyway, this is for you, Gaynor," she said, "you've earned it."

Gaynor opened the bag, and her eyes went wide with the kind of unbridled delight that only too much confectionary can inspire in a woman.

"Terry's Chocolate Orange – loads of the stuff! Oh god, Maggie, that's the best gift I've had all day – I'm going to take it up to the hotel room at the end of the night and gorge on it! Anyway, I've got to go – I need to circulate and let everyone set up their wide angle lenses so they can get a snap of the frock! You two, have a drink, have fun – I'll see you later."

While she spoke, Marco had been busy – using the crutches to heave himself out of the wheelchair, and into a normal one. He looked much bigger, perched there, legs stretched out in front of him.

"You seem pleased with yourself," she said, settling down next to him and taking in his smug grin.

"That's because I am," he replied, leaning the crutches up against the table. "I feel like a strong independent Italian-American man, and I don't need no wheelchair, sister...what I do need, if you don't mind, is a drink. I know you're driving, and I promise not to turn into the annoying drunk person who shouts the same thing in your ear over and over again all night, but is there any chance you could oblige? I could probably stagger to the bar myself – but I'm saving my strength for later. When I take you for a spin on the dancefloor."

"Ha!" she said, standing up again, "I wouldn't recommend it. I'm not much of a dancer, especially in these shoes. I'll probably break your toes, and that's the last thing you need."

"Luckily, I am a fantastic dancer – you can just follow my lead. I'll teach you everything you need to know – and we'll take it nice and slow."

Maggie felt a flare of colour creeping over her cheeks again. She might as well have just coated her whole face in blusher before she came out. Somehow, this man had flipped a switch in her brain that translated everything he said into smut language. She only hoped her brainwaves would go back to normal once he'd left.

"We'll see," she replied, non-committally. "Right. Drinks. *I'll be back*," she added, in a totally rubbish Arnie impression.

Hours later, the night had kicked up to a whole different level. A live band had been on, performing a Mustang Sally that had even had the waiters bopping, and Gaynor and Tony had both made exceedingly rude speeches. Several of the kids had passed out in small, well-dressed heaps around the room, some of them lolling on chairs, others on parents' laps, a couple just completely collapsed under tables, snoring away like exhausted puppies.

The tables were now heaped with paper plates full of chicken bones, half-eaten vol-au-vents, and smudges of chocolate sponge. The staff were lurking around with big black plastic bags, trying to scoop away some of the chaos, and the bar staff probably felt like they needed a spa break to recover from the constant flow of traffic.

Maggie had enjoyed one lovely glass of champagne before switching to the bubbles of fizzy water, and Marco had downed more than a few bottles of Peroni. He'd limped around the room, taken himself to the loo, chatted to pretty much everyone, and hired out his wheelchair for the kids to play with. His plaster cast had been signed by dozens of people, unreadable messages scrawled all over it, along with random love hearts and smiley faces. His hair was all mussed up, and his tie was loose, hanging a few inches lower than it had at the start of the evening. So far, though, he'd managed to stay true to his promise, and not become the drunk person who shouted the same thing in her ear over and over all night.

The DJ, who'd spent the whole break while the band played getting up close and personal with Gaynor's younger sister, was now back on duty – and hitting them with a perfectly timed Christmas hits section.

Maggie and Marco had looked on in absolute hysterics as the bridegroom's father did full-on rock and roll moves to *Jingle Bell Rock*, throwing his wife – who was in her 60s – over his shoulder so hard her skirt flew up and flashed her Spanx. There'd been a mass pogo-ing session to *Fairytale of New York*, where everyone – including them – had called each other scumbags and maggots with great relish. And a heartfelt communal singalong to *I Wish It Could Be Christmas Every Day*.

Maggie had no idea if parties were like this back in Chicago, but Marco seemed to be loving every minute of it – his sparkling hazel eyes drinking it all in; singing (badly) with everyone else, and tapping his good foot along to the music. Even though she was sober, she couldn't remember a time she'd enjoyed a wedding so much. It was partly the atmosphere – Gaynor's extended family were all as loud and lovely as she was – and partly, she knew, because of him. Because she had somebody here sharing it all with her.

By now, she'd normally have made a quiet exit – snuck off home for cocoa and a good book, checking to see if Ellen was in her own bed and breathing; occasionally pausing to put her in the recovery position if she suspected she'd had too much to drink. Then climbing under the covers alone – the way she always had. Despite the fact that she'd managed to get pregnant at a stupidly young age, Maggie had never spent a whole night with a man.

Never cuddled up under a duvet, never spooned, never relaxed into another person's arms to sleep.

On the plus side, she'd also never had to worry about farting in bed, or waking up with bad breath either – her life had been very much her own. Or, to be more accurate, Ellen's.

Tonight, though, she hadn't felt alone. For the whole of the last week, in fact, she'd not felt alone. Because of him – the big, brawny, funny, and strangely sensitive man sitting next to her. She'd had company in the evenings; laughter at work, someone to eat pizza with and drink beer with and watch TV with. Someone to talk to who wasn't a blood relative, who hadn't known her her whole life, and who made her laugh out loud all the time.

There would be a moment, she knew, when she needed to worry about that. To worry about what happened when he left – when he limped back to his own life, thousands of miles away, and she tried to go back to hers. For him, it would probably be a relief – but for her? She wasn't so sure. It was almost as though she'd been given a brief glimpse of how life could be lived; a peek behind the magic curtain of other people's normality.

Still, she decided, as the DJ slowed down the tone with Wham's *Last Christmas*, now was not that time. Now was not for worrying – it was for enjoying. Reality would come crashing back down soon enough.

"Dance, madam?" said Marco, interrupting her thoughts and holding out his hand. "This one is slow enough that even I could manage..."

"No, not this one," she replied, ignoring the hand. Touching him in a non-medical way was asking for trouble, "definitely not this one. And in fact not any of them. You have a broken leg. You're drunk. And I can't dance."

"Aww, you're no fun," he replied, laughing at her. "And why not this one?"

"Because I had my heart broken to this when I was 15. School disco. I was obsessed with a boy called Martin Tellwright – and when the slowies started, he snogged the face off Gemma Long on the dancefloor. I'll never forget it as long as I live."

"Oh no. That's such a sad story. Maybe it's time to make some new memories?"

Maggie looked out at the crowd in front of them. There were plenty of couples all tangled up in each other, including Tony and Gaynor, who'd given up with the dress and changed into a leopard-print playsuit instead. There was a whole lot of swaying going on – the alcohol was really hitting home now – and quite a lot of kissing. Some were probably married, or partners – others, though, like Marco said, were making new memories. If they could remember anything at all the next morning, that was.

The song drew to an end, and the DJ played to his crowd again – *The Power of Love* by Frankie Goes to Hollywood.

Marco hoisted himself upright, and popped just one of his crutches under his arm.

"Come on," he said, gesturing towards the dancefloor. "This is the one. I feel it in my bones. We can make it our special song, and you can laugh at it every time you hear it once I'm gone, remembering the time you looked after that poor hobbling Yank at Christmas."

She looked up at him hesitantly, and he realised she was still not convinced. That the caution she always carried around with her, wore like a cloak, was still firmly in place.

"Maggie, if you don't come with me," he said, "I'll dance alone, and everyone will feel sorry for me. And you know how much I hate people feeling sorry for me. I've mastered the one-legged hop now, I've been practicing all night, and I'm pretty sure I can master the one-legged slow dance. Plus – just for the record, Little Miss Prim, I am definitely *not* drunk. If I was, I'd be dancing on

94

top of the tables, and encouraging strange women to stick cash down my pants."

Maggie rolled her eyes, and muttered something along the lines of 'that's what all the drunk people say', but she did, at last, stand up. She took the hand he was holding out towards her, and together they moved slowly and carefully to the very edge of the dancefloor – Maggie guiding them towards a spot with a wall nearby, in case Marco needed something other than her and one crutch to lean on.

As the song – secretly one of her all-time favourites – floated up and out into the room, Holly Johnson's bittersweet voice urging them all on, she allowed herself to be pulled close to him, his arm clamped firmly around her waist until their bodies met.

She laid her head against his chest and wrapped her arms around him, giving in to the moment, giving in to some basic need to be close to him, feeling herself falling headlong into a black hole of new and frightening sensations. It was just a dance, she told herself. Just one dance in a crowded room – but it left her terrified and thrilled and forced to face the fact that this man could so effortlessly tear her apart at the carefully constructed seams.

His hand came to rest in the small of her back, his fingers fanning out and caressing: gentle, strong, and fiercely sensual as they explored.

She could smell his cologne, and feel his heart thudding as hard as hers, as they swayed, ever so slightly, to the music.

The lights had dimmed, casting flickering shadows all around them, and the only thing she was conscious of was Marco, and the way it felt to be held by him. To feel his fingers touching her, to feel the strength of his thighs crushed into hers. To feel the gentle brush of his lips on her forehead.

He kept a firm hold of her, steadily moving his hips in time to the music, the muscles in his back tensing and releasing beneath the palms of her hands. Without questioning what she was doing, she sighed deeply into his chest, closing her eyes and imagining they were the only two people in the room. In the whole world.

"Hey, Maggie," he whispered, so close she could feel the warmth of his breath. She looked up, into those eyes. Those beautiful hazel eyes gazed back; that delicious mouth curled into a curious half-smile.

She knew what was coming next, and she couldn't stop it. She didn't want to stop it. Hadn't got the will to even try.

He looked at her for a moment, asking the silent question, before leaning down to kiss her. His lips were soft as they touched hers, gentle and tentative, as though he was giving her the chance to change her mind.

When she didn't – when she responded with a ragged breath, her hands trembling as they touched him – the kiss deepened, grew, took on a life of its own.

His hand roamed up over the smooth lines of her back, snaking up into her hair, tangling his fingers in the tresses and pulling her even closer. They'd both stopped dancing now, lost in the kiss – lost in each other. She felt her body moulding into his like water, felt the magic between them spark, felt a sensation like warm liquid flowing through her.

Her fingers touched the side of his face, tracing his cheekbones, his jaw, delving into the dark waves of his hair. Every nerve in her body was tingling, on fire, begging him not to take his lips away from hers. Begging him to kiss her forever, to make her feel like this forever, to never stop.

When he did, when both of them needed to breathe, neither of them had a word to say. They stayed entwined in each other's arms, gazing into each other's eyes as couples swayed and moved around them. Time, it seemed, had stood completely still.

"What just happened?" asked Maggie, breathlessly, eyes wide and shining as reality started to catch up with her.

"I don't really know," replied Marco, stroking the side of cheek with the back of his fingers. "Must have been something to do with the song..."

Chapter 16

"About last night..." Maggie said, as she handed Marco his much-needed mug of steaming caffeine.

"Loved that film," replied Marco, gratefully accepting the coffee and taking one scalding sip. "Demi Moore was hot."

"Not as hot as Rob Lowe."

"Or this coffee."

"That's debatable...anyway. Is everything okay? I don't want anything to be...awkward between us."

That, thought Maggie, was an understatement. They'd driven home in near-silence, both of them aware that they'd crossed a line, changed something that they couldn't change back. She had no idea what he'd been thinking – just that he seemed quieter than normal, more subdued. There was no casual banter, no jokes, no reassuring hand on her knee. It hadn't been tense, exactly – more confused. As though they were both weighing it all up in their minds.

He'd been tired, she knew. Exhausted by his first proper venture into the real world since his injury. Possibly a little more drunk than he thought he was. She'd walked up the path with him, by his side as he took his halting hops along the still frosty paving, and made sure he was safely inside before she returned to the car for the wheelchair.

By the time she got back in, he was lying in bed, staring at the ceiling. She'd hovered in the doorway for a moment, not quite knowing how to react. She might be 34 years old and a mother, but really, she'd had no experiences so far in her life to prepare her for this kind of situation. Maybe if she had, she'd have been able to laugh about it – to chalk it up as one of life's adventures. Dismiss it as just a stolen kiss at a wedding. It happened all the time, she knew. Just not to her.

She'd asked if he needed anything, and was told no. Then as she'd turned to leave, he spoke again.

"Maggie," he said quietly, still fascinated by the cracks in the decorative plasterwork overhead. "Come to Scotland with me."

She'd been so glad he wasn't looking at her when he said it. Her eyes had popped so wide she thought they might fall out of their sockets, and she'd wobbled on her high heels. Right then, she couldn't wait to get away – to retreat to her own territory upstairs, to hide beneath the duvet, surrounded by familiar photos and books and objects. To feel safe and normal and relaxed again. Even one kiss with this man had rattled her so much she couldn't think straight. Taking a road-trip with him – away from her home, her shop, Isabel and Michael's wedding, her small but satisfactory life – sounded as relaxing as walking into a cage of lions coated in sirloin steak.

"Thank you, but no," she'd simply said, before closing the door behind her and wishing she could lock it.

Having spent the whole night sober, she'd gone up to her room with a very large glass of wine in her hand, and the pure intent to knock herself out with alcohol. Everything was too fast. Too confusing. Too different. Ellen and Paddy going away for Christmas; him being here; getting kissed into oblivion at the wedding – it was like a festival of firsts. And she wasn't sure she liked it – wasn't sure her foundations were solid enough to withstand all this sudden change.

The wine had done the trick, and she'd slept surprisingly well – although she had woken up flushed and flustered, at the tail end of a deeply erotic dream that involved the man downstairs and a whole lot of whipped cream. Then the eroticism had been spoiled slightly by the surreal arrival of Nanny McPhee, dressed as a comedy sexy nurse, brandishing a sink plunger – the subconscious brain was a mightily strange place. She realised, as she sat up straight and blinked her groggy eyes open and shut for practice, that Nanny McPhee had actually arrived in the real world – and that was what had woken her.

Wanting to avoid a repeat of the Walking In On Bare Chested Male incident, she'd stayed upstairs, showering, pottering, and generally procrastinating until the nurse had left. She lurked at the top of the steps until she heard the door close behind her, and she knew that Marco would be safely dressed. This was going to be a strange enough morning, without adding semi-nakedness to the mix.

She'd decided, as she pottered and procrastinated, that she was being a baby. That she was over-thinking it all. Making more of it than it deserved. It was just a drunken kiss – Lord knows their's hadn't been the only one going on last night. Everyone was at it – it was that kind of party. And her job, right now, was to help Marco get better – not to treat him like a leper just because he'd followed what was undoubtedly a simple male instinct. Man plus beer plus woman equalled kissing. It had meant nothing – and she needed to be a grown-up about it, go downstairs and clear the air. Put things right between them. There was another wedding to get through today, for goodness' sake.

Now, as she sat opposite him, his damp hair curling around his neck, coffee gripped between his large hands, it didn't seem quite so simple. He wasn't following the script she'd prepared in her head, and the subdued look on his face told her that he'd also been over-thinking it. She didn't know men did that as well.

100

"Okay," he finally said, looking up and meeting her eyes. "I get it. I don't want it to be awkward either – but don't worry, we don't need to have a post-mortem about it. I was drunk. I took advantage of the situation. I kissed you. I'm sorry. Maybe we should just leave it at that."

He sounded weary, regretful. Like he'd woken up with a self-worth problem, as well as a hangover.

"Marco, it wasn't quite like that...it's not as though you turned into a caveman and forced me against my will. You just kissed me. And I...I didn't mind it."

"You didn't *mind* it?" he said, a note of laughter creeping back into his tone. "Wow. That's a glowing recommendation. I see I've not lost my touch with the ladies."

"Okay. Possibly I phrased that a bit wrong. I liked it – just a tiny bit."

"How tiny a tiny bit?" he asked, grasping hold of the opportunity to lighten the tone. "And think of my poor bruised ego before you answer that question."

It was, she said to herself, the single most exciting few minutes of my entire life. The first time I've ever felt like that. The only time I've ever wanted a man more than I've wanted my solitude. The most sensual and stimulating physical contact I've ever experienced – and all of that despite the fact that we were in public. And you were drunk. She wondered how he would react if she said all that out loud. Probably he'd hop as fast as he could to the front door, fearing she was about to go all Kathy Bates in Misery and hobble him to the bed.

"Bigger than a grain of sand but smaller than a Jaffa Cake," she said instead. "Somewhere along those lines...but like you said. We don't need to have a post-mortem. We're both grown-ups. These things happen. I just don't think it should happen again, that's all."

Even as she spoke the words, she wondered how true they were. Part of her *did* want it to happen again, very much. Wanted even more to happen. Wanted to jump right onto that bed with him, and let nature take its course. To see if the magic of that one kiss would translate into the fireworks and fantasy that she suspected it would.

But that, she knew, wouldn't be wise. She liked Marco. Maybe she liked him a bit too much. The whole thing was messing with her head, and she wasn't used to it – she'd built a life for herself and Ellen that worked, and that didn't involve complications like these, for a reason. It was easier, it was safer. He would be out of her life for good within days – and she wished him all the best. Wished him health and happiness and love, and marriage and kids and all the things she could never give him. A repeat performance of last night would just lead them down a path that had no happy endings, certainly not for her.

"All right, Maggie," he replied, putting down his coffee and stretching his arms in the air like some kind of jungle cat. "That's probably for the best. Now, what time is this next wedding? And I tell you now, I'll be furious if there isn't cake."

Chapter 17

Lucy Allsop's wedding was a much different affair than Gaynor's had been. Which made sense – Lucy was a much different woman than Gaynor. The tasteful dress, the under-stated make-up, the beautifully arranged hair – it all screamed class.

It also, thought Maggie, screamed tension – poor Lucy had gone through the service like a sleepwalker, and now stood receiving her guests like she was hosting a funeral, not enjoying the happiest day of her life.

When Maggie and Marco reached the head of the queue, the woman looked about ready to keel over from the stress. A warm smile broke out across her strained features when she saw them approaching, and she held out her hands to Maggie, casting a confused glance at her friend. The friend who looked familiar and yet not, at the same time.

"It's his twin brother," said Maggie, correctly picking up on her thought process. She'd met Rob that time in the shop – and Marco looked enough like him to raise an eyebrow.

"Oh," said Lucy, quietly. "There are two of them?"

She gave a small grin – which looked like her first of the day – and shook his hand.

"I know," replied Maggie. "Who'd have thought it? Are you okay, Lucy?"

She so obviously wasn't okay, it seemed pointless to even ask the question. Maggie was a veteran of these events – and she recognised a Nervous Breakdown Bride when she saw one.

"Umm...yes, of course. It's just been a long day, that's all. The whole family seems to have developed some kind of communal hysteria, and...well, my feet are hurting."

Maggie nodded, and fixed her with a warm smile.

"Can I give you a bit of advice, as a woman who's been to quite a few weddings? Take off the shoes. Have a drink or six. And remember one thing – you're here, today, because you and Josh love each other. You love each other so much, you were ready to make a commitment to spend the rest of your lives together. Everything else – the guests, the in-laws, even, dare I say it, the dress – is irrelevant. A side-show. Today you married the love of your life – and this is just the beginning for you two, not the end. Hold on to that thought, and you'll get through the rest of this, maybe even start to enjoy it. Okay?"

Lucy nodded, some of the tension seeming to drain out of her with the words. Maggie gave her hand a last squeeze, and started to walk on into the reception room. Marco lingered for a moment, and she heard him say: "And by the way – you look absolutely stunning."

Maggie felt a smile tug at the corners of her lips, knowing that at exactly that second, poor Lucy Allsop – now Morgan – would be very prettily blushing as she watched him go.

"You Cavelli men," she said, waiting for Marco to catch up to her, "always seem to know the right thing to say to a woman."

"Well, what can I say? My mama raised me right. And Lucy did look stunning. As well as a little stunned. Can't say that I blame her. This whole thing isn't going to be anything like Gaynor's wedding, is it?" he asked, as they took their seats at the table.

The entire room was pure white, crammed with tasteful arrangements of pale roses and lilies, and equally tasteful classical music was being produced by the bow-tie wearing string quartet in the corner. The other guests looked elegant and affluent, with the types of tan you get from the ski-ing season, and conversation hovered in the air in a low, subdued drone. Nobody was going to get drunk and snog a complete stranger at this party – there'd be no children sliding across the floor, no Christmas songs, and certainly no elderly ladies flashing their Spanx.

"Sadly not," replied Maggie, eagerly taking two glasses of champagne from the tray of a passing waiter. "But at least I can drink at this one."

The ceremony had been held at a large church on the right side of Oxford for Jericho, and the reception was at a very posh hotel near the banks of the river. All of it, especially as the snow had all-but cleared, was within walking distance – or in Marco's case, wheeling distance. Maggie had put on her boots, heels tucked away in a bigger handbag to change into, and they'd strolled all the way – Marco's crutches balanced across his lap, occasionally side-swiping people who got too close. She'd pointed out the colleges like a tour guide as they walked past them, and showed him the first pub she'd got drunk in, and the best chippie in town, and Godwin, where Ellen was studying.

They'd sat together at the back of the crowded church, ignored a few querying glances from guests who disapproved of Marco's jogging pants and shirt combo, and looked on as Lucy did her slow, perfect walk down the aisle. There were gasps of delight as people saw her dress for the first time, and Maggie felt the traditional lift in spirits at their reaction.

"Wow," said Marco, leaning into her. "You made that?"

"All by my little old self," she whispered back, smiling. "Impressed?"

"You bet. It's gorgeous."

"I'll make one for you, if you like," she joked, giggling inside at the thought of how much lace she'd have to stock up to fit around Marco's body.

"Thanks, but I think I'd make a very ugly bride."

Lucy, luckily, had made a beautiful bride – even if she had about as much sparkle to her as an old lettuce left at the bottom of the fridge.

After the service, they'd walked the short distance to the reception, which was currently promising to be the very opposite of a barrel-load of laughs. Maggie could feel a close relationship with the champagne waiters coming on. The posh functions always made her more nervous, and things between her and Marco still hadn't settled onto an entirely even keel. They were both trying, but they also were both tense. Not quite back to the same level of easy banter that they'd enjoyed previously.

Hopefully nothing, she thought, draining her glass, that time and an acceptably small amount of alcohol couldn't solve. She followed her own advice to Lucy, and kicked off the shoes under the table. Marco was gazing around at the other guests, a slight frown on his face.

"What is it?" she said immediately. "Are you in pain?"

"Nah," he said, turning back to her. "I'm like Superman. I don't feel pain. I was just thinking that this reminds me of home – of the things I don't like about home, anyway. Mainly I go my own way, but I've had to attend a lot of events like this one. Society things. Cavelli things. Gatherings, my mother always calls them. Rob's better at it than me – or at least he is now he's emerged from the black hole. He's the head of the company, he's the one who has to do most of the gladhanging and schmoozing – I'm just the head of legal. But I do have to do it – and it never feels right. It's like this – too many people thinking more about what everyone else is wearing than why they're here."

"I know what you mean," Maggie replied, looking around her. "The clothes in this room are probably worth more than my house. I hope you can forgive me for being a slattern and wearing the same dress two days in a row."

"I can forgive any woman who actually uses the word 'slattern' in a real life sentence," he said, grinning at the expression. "And you still look better than most of these bozos. How long do we have to stay here for? Can we escape? Do something more fun, like douse ourselves in battery acid?"

Maggie thought it over. Looked at the menu. Looked at the other guests. Looked at the bottles of expensive wine sitting on the table in front of them.

"We need to stay to eat our twice baked goat's cheese and walnut soufflé, and our pan-fried poussin, and maybe to drink a couple of glasses of wine between us. Then I reckon we could build a tunnel and emerge in a pub somewhere, if that's what you fancy? I could take you to my local. See if you can throw darts while balancing on one leg."

"Even with the darts, I fancy it a whole lot more than twice baked goat's cheese and walnut soufflé, for sure."

"Great. Then we have a plan. Look...there's Lucy..." she said, gesturing with her head in the direction of the bride. The bride who was walking – unashamedly barefoot – towards the top table, one hand clasped in her husband's, the other clasped around a champagne glass, and with a beaming smile on her now radiant face.

Chapter 18

"This," said Maggie, sitting down on the bench next to Marco, "is one of my favourite places in a whole city full of favourite places."

"And I can see why," replied Marco, gazing out across the river. She'd brought him here, to this secluded spot, straight after their pan-fried poussin. Lucy had looked a lot happier by the time they made their excuses and left, blatantly lying about Marco's medical needs, and after they had indeed finished off a bottle of wine between them.

"Is this the Thames?" he asked, mesmerised by the way the moonlight danced in glittering silver stripes over the gently flowing water. It was after six, and night had fallen. The place was deserted, apart from the occasional dog walker, or hardy rower out for cold-weather practice.

"Technically yes, but it's known as the Isis. Over there, on the far bank, are the boathouses – where the colleges do their rowing. And over there, in the distance with all the lights, is Christ Church. Between them, if we were walking on the other side, there's a big meadow with cows in it."

"Cows? In the middle of the city? Are you messing with me?"

"No! I'll take you there some time, and show you – they're Longhorns as well, they'd be right at home in Texas. And I'll take you to Magdalen, and show you the deer park. This isn't like other cities."

"So I'm gathering. You English are crazy. But...it's beautiful, isn't it? So peaceful."

"I know. I thought we could both do with a bit of peace while we let our soufflé settle. I've come here a lot over the years – just sat here, watching the seasons change. It's completely different in summer – full of tourists. Or in May, when it's Eights Week, it's like one giant party – all the colleges rowing against each other, all the boathouses open, everyone tanked up on Pimms, all the parents down for the occasion. It's fun – but I like it like this. When all you can see is the moonlight, and the frost on the grass, and all you can hear is the river. It's a little bit magical."

"Like something from Alice in Wonderland," he said, his smile glinting white in the darkness.

"Funny you should say that – Christ Church is where the real Alice lived, don't you know?"

"I didn't know, no – you are a regular mine of information, aren't you, Maggie?"

She nodded, grinning back at him.

"I am. Completely. Go on, test me..."

Maggie was giggling, and it was a totally new sound for her as far as Marco was concerned. He'd seen her after a few beers before, but never quite this...merry. He wasn't an idiot – he'd realised she was nervous around him; that he'd over-stepped the mark the night before. That he'd scared her, no matter how much she tried to be grown-up about it. That the wine she'd been chugging down so quickly had at least something to do with that.

He knew he should probably regret it – regret doing anything that drove a wedge between them – but somehow, he couldn't bring himself to. That kiss...the way she'd felt in his arms, the way she'd felt melting against his body; so soft, so responsive. So very surprised by what they'd both experienced. Her wide, shocked eyes as they finally pulled apart. He'd kissed a lot of women – and none of them had affected him quite like that.

He'd spent the whole journey back to the house wondering what to do about it. Usually, he'd know exactly what to do about it – keep up the good work and persuade her into bed with him. But Maggie was different. And he was different when he was with Maggie. None of the usual rules seemed to apply here – he was on completely unknown ground.

Whether that was a good thing or a bad thing, he wasn't sure. But he at least wanted to perhaps find out – unlike the woman in question. She'd made it clear it was a mistake, that it should never be repeated. She'd dipped her toe in the water and recoiled in terror.

But now, here she was. Snuggled up against him, both of them wrapped up in warm winter coats, sitting on a cold bench on a frosty riverbank in the moonlight. Giggling away, and asking him to test her knowledge. Maybe, he thought, this was his chance – his chance to find out a little bit more about how she felt, about what she was thinking. Or, if things didn't go to plan, a whole lot more about the history of Oxford.

"Okay. Let's test each other," he said, reaching out and taking one of her hands in his. They both had gloves on, but it still felt like the right thing to do. "This is a game I used to play with Rob, when we were kids. We'd take it in turns asking questions, and then both have to answer at the same time. It was usually stuff about which girls we liked at school; what we wanted for Christmas, what we'd said to the Father when we were dragged along to confession...that kind of thing."

Maggie shifted slightly, looking up at him with a frown.

"That sounds a bit more personal than asking me what year the first Boat Race took place, Marco...are you trying to take advantage of me because I'm a bit tiddly?"

"Tiddly! Another excellent word, Maggie. And maybe, yeah – though I promise I won't throw you over my shoulder or anything."

"You wouldn't be able to, not in your condition..." she replied. "But go on then. If you insist. Go easy on me though. I'm not used to people actually being interested in what I say – it could all go disastrously wrong."

"I'm always interested in what you say, and I promise to be gentle with you..."

He gazed off into the distance. Go easy on her, he thought, trying to think of a good one to start off with...something that wouldn't freak her out, something funny, something they could both laugh about.

"Okay. Now – this is the question, then we both answer on the count of three, all right? No silences, no refusals, no kick to the nuts – you have to answer. And expand after if you want to."

She nodded in response, the bobble of her green woollen hat bouncing up and down in time with her head.

"Here goes. Get ready – here it comes, Maggie. What is...." he paused dramatically, "your favourite colour?"

They both counted out together – one, two, three – and Marco said 'blue' and Maggie said 'green'. As soon as she'd gotten the word out, she burst into laughter, poking him in the ribs with her elbow.

"You swine! I thought there was something serious coming then, I was terrified!"

"Well, I can't promise they won't get harder. Right. Next one. After three, now, both together: who's the sexiest member of the British Royal Family and why?"

Again, they counted to three.

"Prince Harry!" said Maggie.

"Camilla!" said Marco. "Why Harry?"

"Because he's a member of the ginger master race. Why Camilla?"

"Are you crazy?" he asked, feigning bewilderment, "that woman is a stone cold fox!"

His reply made Maggie actually snort with laughter so un-lady-like she apologised for it. She was still shaking by the time Marco laid a hand on her leg, and told her to get ready for the next one.

"Question number three coming at ya...how old were you when you had your first proper date?"

"14," said Maggie.

"11," said Marco. "Bowling with Virginia Rafferty. She pinned me up against a wall and stuck her tongue down my throat. It was the beginning of a beautiful relationship."

"Uggh. Sounds horrible – how long did you date her for?"

"For a whole seven days. It was the longest week of my life... okay. You ready for the next one? This is a humdinger."

"Go on, I'm ready for anything," she said, eyes glinting with amusement.

"When was the last time," he said slowly, building up the tension as he had before, "you had sex?"

He saw Maggie's eyes widen, and heard the lacklustre way she counted along to three, and thought that maybe this one had been a mistake. It was meant to be silly. Slightly risqué. Lighthearted. At least that was the intention – but the look on her face told him otherwise. Told him that he'd unintentionally taken a mis-step, right into a minefield he hadn't seen coming. Shit. Too late now.

"Last month," said Marco, not choosing to expand on that. It wouldn't be polite, for all sorts of reasons – not least of which was the despondent look on his friend's face.

"May 1996," said Maggie in a whisper a moment later. She immediately broke eye contact with him, and stared instead at her lap, head bowed, shaking her hair so that it shielded her face. He'd seen girls do that before. It often meant they were embar-rassed, or worried, or even crying. Maybe, in this case, all three.

Aah, damn, he thought, what've I gone and done now? And what can I do to make it better?

He wasn't dumb. He could do basic math, and he knew what her whispered confession meant. 1996 was the year she got pregnant with Ellen. And from what she'd told him, the relationship with Ellen's father had never gone beyond that one initial accident. Could that really be true, he wondered? That this amazing, beautiful, sensual woman had only ever had sex one time in her entire life – sex that resulted in turning her whole world upside down? Jeez. No wonder she was nervous around him. She must feel like she was swimming with sharks. And now he completely understood why their kiss had left her so amazed – it had had the same effect on him, and he wasn't exactly a stranger to the ways of the flesh.

He put his arm around her shoulder, and pulled her in tight. He was careful to keep his touch comforting, reassuring. No sly strokes. No touching her hair. No kisses to her forehead. Friendly, supportive uncle all the way.

"I know," she said, leaning into him, her voice slightly muffled against the padding of his jacket. "It's pathetic, isn't it? I've never told anybody. It's not the kind of conversation you have with your father or your teenaged daughter, and the friends I have in my life have always assumed I was...you know...normal. Active but independent. In reality, life went nuts after Ellen was born. Her. My dad. Then work. I wasn't exactly in the mood to meet men. I didn't plan it like that – it just never happened, apart from that one time. And I was so drunk I can't even remember it! How sad is that??"

"It is pretty sad," he said, nuzzling into her hair before he realised what he was doing. "It's sad because you've missed out. Because you've been lonely. Because so long has gone by that something natural and joyous must all look like a foreign land to you. But

113

it's not pathetic, Maggie – nothing about you is pathetic. And it will change. You've said it yourself – everything is changing right now. Your life isn't over – it's just beginning."

"Ha! That's easy for you to say," she replied. "You had sex last month! You were practically having sex with Virginia Rafferty when you were only 11! I bet you have loads of women back home; I bet you've had loads of great relationships...I bet you've been in love, at least."

Marco paused before he replied. He should tell her the truth. Except he wasn't quite sure what the truth was any more – he felt like he was stranded on ever-shifting sands.

"Okay, that's the next question," he said, "on the count of three – have you ever been in love?"

"There's no need for the countdown, Marco, not for me – obviously I haven't!" said Maggie, still tucked away in his coat, her words punctuated by small sniffles.

"Well...hey, me neither," he said, raising her face up to his so he could look into her eyes. Eyes that were, as he'd suspected, glittering with tears. The wine. The tension. Last night. Now the questions. It had all been a bit too much for her.

"So you're not so pathetic, are you?" he asked. "I might have had more sex than you, but I've never been in love either. It just never happened. Never even came close. If you're a loser, Maggie, then I'm right up there with you. And at least you have Ellen. At least you have your beautiful daughter – and anyone who created her can't possibly be pathetic. It's not genetically possible."

That, at least, managed to coax a small, sad smile out of her. He pulled off his glove, and tucked stray locks of red hair behind her ears.

"See?" he said, stroking her cheeks, wiping away the tears. "you're way ahead of the game. I don't have kids. I've created nothing. Not like your masterwork."

"Yes. You're right. She is a masterwork, isn't she? In an evil kind of way. Thanks for that. Can I ask you a question now?" she said quietly, the tears finally stemmed. "And can I apologise for the fact that I've probably got snot on your jacket?"

"Yes on both counts, sweetheart – go for it," he replied.

"Do you even want kids?"

Ah. She'd caught him in a big question. One of the biggest. One he didn't really know the answer to. He felt those sands shift beneath him yet again.

"In all honesty, Maggie, I don't know. I never had any big burning desire to go forth and multiply. But seeing how happy Luca has made Rob did kind of change that; heck, even seeing Ellen changed that. So the answer is...maybe. Probably. One day. When I meet the right woman, and when I know I'll be bringing a child into the right environment. Or when my mother forces me to – whichever comes first. What about you? I know now why you've never had any more – I'm a biology whizz kid like that – but you're still young. There's still plenty of time for you."

She pulled away from him suddenly, springing to her feet like her ass was on fire. She used her gloves to wipe her face, and tugged her hat more firmly down around her ears. Looked like question time was over.

"I've had enough of this game," she said, her tone falsely bright. "We've got a pub to go to."

Chapter 19

The pub was packed. Maggie had taken a peek inside, wondering how she was going to get a wheelchair through the crowds and also wondering if they should just give up and go home. Lord knew she was ready for bed anyway.

She'd kept the conversation light between them on the walk back to Jericho, embarrassed and awkward after her unplanned confession. Pointing out the sights, making lame jokes, anything at all other than face up to the fact that she'd told this man her deepest, darkest secret. Or one of them at least.

Marco had played along, bless him, even though she knew he must be buzzing with questions. He wouldn't be human if he wasn't – but he seemed to recognise her need for privacy. Her need to ignore the whole thing, and retreat back into the casually guarded stance that had defined her whole emotional life as an adult.

She was grateful for that, and not surprised. He was far more sensitive than his bulk and brazenly male persona suggested. He was also, she noticed, looking colder by the second. It was all right for her – the brisk trot through the slushy streets, pushing the chair, had kept her temperature up. He, though, was shivering slightly, and gazing in hope at the pub door as she let it swing shut behind her.

"Please," he said, "tell me there's room at the inn."

"Ha," Maggie replied, chewing her lip as she thought, "we might need to find a kindly stable owner. Or...we could leave the chair outside, if you can manage on the crutches? I'm sure someone will take pity on a poor crippled man and offer us a seat."

"And I can cry on demand if necessary," he said, already clambering up and out of the chair, propping the crutches under his arms and steadying himself. He took a deep breath as Maggie folded it up and hid it behind the pub door. Just in case anyone took it for a joy ride.

"Let's do this," he announced, gesturing towards the entrance with one upraised crutch. "I so need a drink."

Maggie went first, clearing a path through the warm bodies, saying her hellos to the people she knew and scanning the room for a space. The temperature was tropical, and the juke box was on full blast – some kind of 80s rock tune she recognised but couldn't name. It was an old-fashioned pub, all dark wood and real-ale pumps behind the long bar, and pulled in a crowd every night of the week. Even when the students went home, there were enough locals to keep it busy – especially at Christmas, when everyone had an excuse to be out.

Marco followed behind, smiling at strangers and hopping carefully as Maggie's 'excuse me's opened up a passageway to the back room.

"Oh! Bugger!" he heard her say, as she came to a sudden stop. He peered over her shoulder, into the room, wondering what it was that had brought her to a halt.

Straight away, he saw what it was – sitting there, at a small copper-topped table laden down with pint glasses, was Ellen. Right next to her granddad. Both of them were staring at Maggie accusingly; Ellen with a mighty frown across her forehead.

"Shit..." he muttered, leaning in close behind Maggie's body. "It's too late to run. You've been rumbled."

117

"I know," she murmured back, waving at them and plastering a fake smile on her face. "But maybe they've not talked about Christmas yet...maybe it'll be all right..."

As they approached the table, Ellen shuffling along to make room for Marco, and Paddy finding a spare stool for Maggie to perch on, he suspected that was incredibly wishful thinking. These two had the look of people who'd been settled in for a while – and weren't exactly delighted to see Maggie.

The woman herself was fidgeting around on the stool, fishing in her bag for her purse, planning to make a very quick dash to the bar to get the drinks in. It might, she thought hopefully, be extremely busy and take a very long time to get served. And there was always the chance that she could get abducted by aliens on the way there. Even a severe session with an anal probe would be more fun than this.

"What can I get everyone?" she said brightly, brandishing a £20 note in the air.

"Well," said Ellen, narrowing her eyes at her mother in a way that even made Marco feel nervous. "You can get me a pint of cider, granddad'll have a Guinness, and for you I'd suggest a double truth serum and tonic."

Maggie froze, her gulp audible even over the sound of the juke box and the chattering crowds.

"Did you really think we wouldn't talk to each other between now and Christmas, mum?" asked Ellen, gesturing at Paddy, who was sitting with his hands folded across his huge beer belly, looking on like an elderly Buddha.

"I went round to Granddad's this afternoon to ask if I could borrow his wheelie suitcase for my trip. When I got there he told me he was using it, for a cruise to the Canaries with Jim. And – because we're not both completely brain dead – we realised that you'd been fibbing. Letting him think you'd be spending Christmas with me. And letting me think you'd be spending Christmas with him. What the fuck, mum? You *know* we wouldn't want to leave you on your own!"

She was bristling with annoyance by the time she finished her speech, leaning forward and glaring at Maggie with anger she didn't even bother to try and hide. Maggie knew her well enough to realise what her hostility was hiding – the fact that she was hurt. Upset. Worried about leaving her mother alone, and guilty at even wanting to. It was exactly the same set of emotions she'd hoped to avoid, and epically failed at dodging.

Her granddad patted Ellen on the hand, and made gentle hushing noises to stop the flow.

"What she means, love," he said, "is that we don't want you to be on your own. That we wished you'd told us, rather than us finding out like this. We love you, and we'd rather spend Christmas with you than go away. We've talked about it, before you got here, and we've both decided that we're cancelling our trips. That we'll have a nice, normal family do – all together, like we always have had."

"No," replied Maggie, as firmly as she could. "That's not going to happen. I'm sorry I didn't mention it, but it all happened pretty quickly. Ellen told me first, and that was fine – and then you, dad. And that was fine too. It still is. I want you both to go, and both to enjoy yourselves. I'm a grown woman, and I don't need you two to babysit me. I have my own life."

"We all know that's not true," Ellen snapped, tapping her fingertips on the top of the table, fizzing with energy. "And much as it pains me to use the L-word, he's right, we do both love you – and we won't leave you on your own at this time of year. We're staying, and you're just going to have to deal with it. Paris probably sucks anyway."

Marco watched the emotions play over Maggie's face in response to Ellen's words. The content was sweet – but the delivery was sour. He knew Maggie well enough by now to guess what she was feeling: touched, upset, guilty, trapped. Especially trapped.

He leaned forward slightly, interrupting their conversation, and sliding his hand around under the table to grasp hold of Maggie's trembling fingers.

"There's no need to change your plans," he said, waiting for a few seconds until he was sure he had Ellen and Paddy's full attention. "She won't be alone."

All three of them looked at him expectantly. Only Maggie might have had even a slight idea about what was coming next, and she frowned at him as she anticipated it.

"She won't be alone, because she's coming to Scotland. With me."

Chapter 20

"Mu-um!" Ellen hollered up the stairs. It was the day she was leaving for London, and she was up and about uncharacteristically early, doing all the packing she'd more characteristically failed to do the night before. And she was obviously keen to share the joy.

Maggie glanced at the clock through foggy eyes. Just gone 7am. Nice. She wiped the sleep from her lids, and fought the urge to hide under the covers as she heard Ellen's footsteps barrelling up the stairs.

The door burst open, and her daughter stood there, hands on hips and hair akimbo. Aaagh, thought Maggie, peeking out at her from behind the duvet. Too much energy!

"Mum!" she repeated, striding forward and tugging the sheets away from her still-comatose parent. "You need to wake up. Two very essential things to sort out. First – and most important – can I take your hair straighteners with me? Mine aren't working. Well, they are, but I seem to have got a load of chewing gum stuck on them and I don't think that would be a very Parisian look."

"Yeah, fine," mumbled Maggie, accepting defeat and sitting upright, leaning against the headboard and fantasising about a coffee fairy who might emerge in place of a sparky teenager. "What else? You said two things?"

"Oh yes. I did. Nanny McPhee just called – she's not coming. Her husband's got shingles and she says she can't make it. There'll be a replacement sorted by the agency for tomorrow, but you're going to have to rough it for today. Marco's awake – says to tell you don't worry, there's coffee waiting downstairs. Which *I* made, selfless creature that I am. Right...busy busy! Can you drop me at the station later?"

"Maybe," Maggie replied, yawning, stretching, and still coming to terms with the Nanny McPhee sickie shocker. "Depends on what mood I'm in."

Ellen poked her sharply in the ribs, then cackled, jumped to her feet, and jogged out of the room.

Lord, thought Maggie, waiting for her body and mind to achieve any kind of symbiosis, to have that much life flowing through your veins first thing in the morning...it didn't seem right. It was like Ellen had taken both their shares. The child was a parasite in human form.

The house, she knew, was definitely going to feel a lot quieter once that wonderfully loud parasite had left it. Jacob's mum had been lovely on the phone, responding to questions Maggie didn't even know she had, putting her mind completely at rest that her daughter would be safe. She'd seen Taken a few too many times to not have some doubts about letting her 18-year-old daughter loose in Paris – but it sounded like they'd be well escorted all the way, met at the airport, driven to their apartment, and looked after for the whole week. Marco had insisted on contributing to the Euro fund; Maggie had bought Ellen her own wheelie suitcase, and all was going according to plan. The only thing left was the bon voyage later in the morning, which would undoubtedly eat its way through a few packs of hankies.

But first, she thought, as she clambered out of bed and scrabbled for her slippers, we need to sort my hobbling houseguest out. Nanny McPhee's brush with illness couldn't have come at a worse time – today was the day he was giving his lecture at the Institute. He didn't seem at all nervous – not like she would have been at the thought of speaking in front of hundreds of people – but he'd probably want to be clean, at least. Maybe she could just wheel him into the garden naked and hosepipe him down, like a muddy St Bernard.

Getting quickly dressed, Maggie made her way downstairs, ignoring the sharp swear words coming from Ellen's room. If she was sitting on that new suitcase and busting the zip, she didn't want to know about it.

As she walked into the living room, she saw Marco, holding out a mug of steaming black coffee. She nodded good morning, not yet feeling capable of vocalising it, and took it from him before sitting down.

"She told you?" Marco asked, raising an eyebrow quizzically.

"Yes. It's not a disaster. I can just get you what you need and… leave you to it. Unless you want me to come in and scrub your back for you."

"Only if you apply fake warts before you do it," replied Marco, grinning. "That's what I look forward to most every morning. But – I was wondering…I'm much steadier on my feet now, stronger all together. How about we go back to my flat before the lecture? If you drive me there, I could actually take a proper shower. Wash my own hair. All that big boy stuff. It's on the ground floor, so that wouldn't be a problem. I could water my prize orchids and feed my pet chinchillas while I was there."

"You don't have any prize orchids, or pet chinchillas, do you?" she asked, used to his sense of humour by now.

"No, but I *would* really like a shower."

Maggie pondered the issue as she sipped her coffee. Logistically, she could manage it – take him there, then on to the lecture by nine. Drop him off. Come back for Ellen, take her to the train station for ten. Call into the shop to collect Isabel's dress, now she'd made the final adjustments – taking it in yet again, as the poor woman had lost even more weight. She could give that a final steaming and leave it ready for them to collect the day after. The two bridesmaids' dresses had already been finished and taken.

It could all be done in time to collect Marco at 12. Chaotic, but possible. And within a few days her life would be entirely her own again anyway – she might as well make the most of the chaos while it lasted.

"Well, I could do that," she replied once she'd thought it through. "But don't you need to keep your cast dry?"

"I do," he said, staring at it with something resembling hatred. "But I've been thinking about that. I could wrap it up in a trash bag, and maybe tape it together at the top and bottom to stop the water getting in? What do you think?"

"Yes. That could work. We could rig something up. Well...are you ready now? I have a few things to do today, and I need to see Ellen off, so the sooner we make a move, the better."

He nodded, and immediately climbed off the bed and onto his crutches, hopping around the room and gathering his notes together.

He looked utterly thrilled, and it made Maggie realise how hard all of this must have been for him. The lack of independence. Not even having access to a shower he could use himself. Enduring Nanny McPhee every morning. Being completely reliant on other people all the time. And mostly – apart from the occasional lapse – he'd dealt with it well. Hadn't even complained when he'd been sucked into family dramas, dragged along to wedding dress fittings, paraded at parties, and had her crying on his shoulder about her lack of a love life.

When all this was over, she'd go and buy him one of those toy medals they gave out to kids on school sports' days – he'd earned it just by digging her out of the holiday hole she'd buried herself in with her dad and Ellen.

They'd eventually accepted the 'she's going to Scotland' story, even though it wasn't true. Partly because Marco had been so convincing – and partly because they wanted to. It was easier for everyone. They never needed to know that she was planning to stay at home; that she couldn't go to Scotland with Marco, for several reasons.

One reason was simple – she wanted to go to Isabel and Michael's wedding on Christmas Eve. Others were...less simple. More to do with the strangeness of how close they'd become in such a short space of time. With the way he made her feel; with how that kiss had made her feel.

With the fact that when she was with him, she felt happier, more content. Both more at peace with the world and more excited by it. All of which might have been a good thing if it wasn't so temporary – but it was. He would be leaving. He would be going to Scotland, and then to Chicago, and then disappearing from her life. He wasn't a permanent part of her existence – and spending Christmas with him would just make it harder to say goodbye.

Still, the lie had served its purpose. Her dad had left for the cruise terminal at Southampton the day before, giddy as a school kid with his friend Jim, already using the early Christmas present she'd given him – an engraved hip flask that he'd filled with rum. And Ellen was back to being acidically excited and abusing innocent suitcases. Neither of them, as far as Maggie could tell, suspected she was fibbing yet again.

She was relieved about that, and even, she had to admit to herself, slightly looking forward to spending a few days alone. Everything had been so hectic and confusing recently. It would be a relief to get her house back to normal, get her life back to normal. Get her emotions back to normal. It would be dull, but dull could be good. Dull could be her friend, she decided. It had worked so far in life, anyway.

She finished the coffee as quickly as she could, and helped Marco pack up his laptop before walking into the kitchen to get bin bags, duct tape and scissors. She piled them all into a rucksack, feeling like she was assembling a serial killer kit, and then pulled on her coat and boots.

Shouting a probably-unheard goodbye to Ellen, she helped Marco down the path and into the car, glancing back at the house as she went.

The streets were clear of snow now, but there was still a solid patch of white in her front garden, untouched apart from the small tracks made by birds. The inflatable Santa in the house opposite was looking a little the worse for wear, folding over in the middle, as though he'd eaten a few too many mince pies and felt a bit sick. The reindeers had woollen scarves tied around their necks, and a badly deformed snowman was squatting between them with a carrot sticking out of his face.

Just a few more days, she thought, climbing into the car, and it'll all be over. The insanity will come to a close, and everything can go back to its normal, bleak, January self.

As she slid the door shut and turned to Marco to check he was belted in, she realised he was humming to himself, staring out of the window at the forlorn Santa. She paused a moment, trying to catch the familiar tune. After a few more absent-minded hums, she got it.

"Do you wanna build a snowman?" she said, laughing out loud. This big, beefy, macho man was sitting there, singing a song from a kids' movie. Priceless.

He grimaced, and shrugged broad shoulders.

"What can I say? I have a two-year-old nephew. That damn film was on repeat back in the flat for days on end. I could probably recite the whole script if I tried."

"Maybe you should do that at your lecture instead," she said, starting up the car and heading them towards the Woodstock Road, and Marco's flat. The mythical land of showers, orchids, and pet chinchillas.

They were there within minutes, and Maggie looked on curiously as she pulled up outside. It was one of the old Victorian villas, with a communal garden and carpark, set right back off the road. Some of them were still grand family houses, but a lot had been converted, like this one, for temporary lets or student accommodation.

"Home sweet home..." mumbled Marco as he fumbled with the keys, opening the door into the hallway. He used his good foot to kick away a pile of junk mail, and led Maggie inside. "Or at least until the end of the month."

The living room was huge, a massive bay window looking out onto the front garden. Maggie glanced around, keenly interested in the way Marco had been living before he crash landed in Jericho with her. They walked through to the en-suite bedroom, and Maggie realised that Leah had obviously been in and sprinkled some fairy dust – all of the clothes had been cleared away, the bed had been made, and there was a strand of golden tinsel tied around the headboard that she was guessing wasn't exactly Marco's style.

Not, she reminded herself as she sat down on the bed, that she knew what Marco's style was – and this flat, sterile and musty, wasn't going to give her any clues. Apart from a few tattered paperback copies of Thomas the Tank Engine on the bedside cabinet – either some easy night-time reading or leftovers from Luca's stay – there was little here that was personal. It looked like what it was – a nice apartment, rented for a month's working holiday. When he handed back the keys and left for good, there would be no sign at all that he'd ever been there.

Maggie wondered absently if it would be the same with her house. Once the hired bed and the recliner had gone, once the tangible signs of Marco had all been removed, would he be gone forever? Or would he linger, like a hobbling ghost, forever on the edge of her vision as she tried to settle back into her everyday life?

"Okay," he said, standing in front of her and dragging her back to the here and now. "How do we do this? Have you got the stuff?"

Maggie patted the serial killer kit by her side, and nodded. It was a good question – how did they do this? Could he do it on his own? Or was she going to be an accessory to the crime?

His eyes met hers, direct and questioning, and she felt a slow blush start to spread up her neck and towards her cheeks. View him like a patient, she told herself. Channel your inner Nanny McPhee. Forget the fact that it's the Hot Papa from the Park. That it's the Man with the Tux. That it's the man who made you quite literally weak at the knees at Gaynor's wedding. He's just a friend who needs your help.

"I think," she said eventually, breaking eye contact and extracting the bin bag and the tape, "that you should take your clothes off."

"Maggie, I thought you'd never ask," he replied, his tone light and playful. She kept her gaze averted as he leaned back against the edge of the bed for support, and used both hands to pull his T-shirt over his head. She continued to be fascinated by her roll of tape as he sat down next to her, and tugged off his jogging pants.

Finally, when she couldn't avoid it any more, she knelt down in front of him. He'd kept his boxers on, thank the Lord, but she was still confronted by a huge expanse of bare male flesh. More than she'd ever seen in real life before, that was certain.

Long legs stretched out in front of him; powerful thighs, tanned skin. All attached to a muscular torso that she'd seen before, but still made her hands tremble. It was one thing knowing a man was big when he had his clothes on – it was entirely different having him sitting there before you practically in the buff.

Keeping her eyes on the plaster cast, she managed to fumble out the plastic bag, and wrap it around his knee.

"Hold that there for me," she said, grabbing up the tape and peeling back a length. She needed to cut it, but her fingers were shaking so much she wasn't sure she could handle the scissors. Instead, she bit the edge until it broke, and used it to secure the top end of the bin bag, and then the lower part, around his ankle. The tape was yellow and the bag was black, and his leg looked like a huge, shiny bumble bee.

She patted it down, checking everything was safely covered, and tried to ignore the fact that her breathing was suddenly too fast, too desperate. Entirely possibly too audible. It would be so very easy, she knew, to leave that hand there. To let her fingers drift up to his thigh. To touch and stroke and appreciate every masculine curve of that body. To topple him down onto that neatly made bed, and climb on there with him.

She might be inexperienced, but she wasn't an idiot. She knew he found her attractive, for some strange reason. From the corner of her eye, she realised there were things going on in those boxer shorts that made studying the carpet especially important, and things going on in her own body that she had no idea what to do with. It was like being possessed by an especially horny demon.

"There," she said, giving the wrapping a final pat and jumping to her feet. "All done."

She turned around quickly, hoping to avoid his eyes, to avoid any complications. To avoid seeing the invitation that she suspected was posted all over his face. It was just too much.

"All righty," he replied, quietly, before she heard him getting to his feet. Heard him grab the crutches. Heard him hopping away towards the shower. And finally, much to her relief, heard the sound of the water flowing – and Marco singing about snowmen.

Maggie flopped backwards onto the bed, staring at the ceiling and waiting for the flames that had consumed her face to fade away.

At least, she told herself, he was lucky enough to get straight into a cold shower.

Chapter 21

Maggie trotted up the imposing colonnaded steps to the Law Institute, following the signs for the reception and wishing she was better dressed. Jeans and T-shirts were just fine for Jericho – but here, she felt like a bag lady begging for spare change.

She'd tried to run a brush through her hair, and then spent the next five minutes trying to remove the brush from her hair when it got too tangled to budge. Maybe she should have just left it, sticking out in its pink plastic glory, and confirmed her status as someone in need of kindly police assistance.

It had been a hectic morning, and the last thing she felt like doing was walking into a room full of successful professional people who probably looked like they modelled for Stylish Lawyer Monthly on the side.

Waving Ellen off had been harder than she imagined. Even her normally resilient daughter seemed to have switched off her sarcasm button for the occasion, and the two of them had stood hugging on the platform for long, weepy minutes as the train pulled in.

"You'll be all right won't you? In Scotland?" Ellen had asked, swiping ferociously away at her tears as though it offended her to be caught out displaying some humanity.

"Course I will, silly," replied Maggie, "you just concentrate on having a good time, and learning as many French swear words as possible. Text me when you've landed, and call me on Christmas Day. And don't worry about me – I'll be fine with Marco."

Ellen had raised an eyebrow at that, a suggestive smirk settling on her lips.

"Who'd have thought it, eh?" she'd asked. "That bloke you were perving over in the park – a wearer of festive knitwear, no less – has ended up as your hot Christmas date. Weird."

"It is weird, but it's not a date," said Maggie, rooting in her purse for an extra £10 note to hand over. Motherhood – the gift that kept on giving.

"Whatever you say, mum," answered Ellen, pocketing the cash and giving her a quick last hug. "Au revoir – and don't do anything I wouldn't do!"

Maggie had watched the train pull out, waving frantically at the window as her daughter's face got smaller and smaller, wondering if she could chase it all the way to Paddington. When it had completely disappeared from sight, she wrapped her arms around herself – staving off the cold, staving off more tears – and trekked back to the car park.

She knew that later, when the Ellen-shaped dust had settled, she'd be lost. She'd miss her so much, even if recently she'd only seen her for brief bouts of abuse each day. But right then, she'd decided, she had to hold it together. Get herself back to the shop. Get Isabel's dress ready. And get the car round to the Institute to collect her non-Christmas non-date.

Neither she nor Marco had talked much on the journey from his flat to the lecture hall. She'd settled on the leather sofa in the living room after he'd taken himself off for a shower, knowing he could call her if he needed help, but hoping like hell he wouldn't. Seeing him undressed the once had been quite enough. She didn't need to add 'fresh from the shower' to the image bank as well. She'd listened as he hopped around, uttering the odd expletive as he dressed himself, but never once shouting her name.

When he walked back in – wearing a fresh white shirt, a pale blue tie, and his now traditional black running pants – she'd pretended to be reading a copy of the local free sheet that had been poked through the letterbox. There'd been a mini Christmas crime wave – wreaths getting stolen from front doors. What was the world coming to?

"Ready to go?" she'd asked, getting up and clutching the car keys.

"As I'll ever be," he'd replied. It was pretty much the last thing either of them said, right until she dropped him off at the ground-floor disabled access, and escorted him in with his laptop bag and notes.

They'd been met there by a woman who looked like she never got her hairbrush stuck in her tangles. Introducing herself with some impossibly chic European sounding name, she'd gazed at Marco like he was hot chocolate fudge cake, and taken him away on her stupidly high heels, leaving Maggie standing there like the shabby spare part she was.

The same woman, she noticed as she crept into the reception room, was with him now. The rest of the crowd was a mixed bag – some very sharp suits, some perfectly tailored dresses, but also a scattering of jeans and hoodies from the post-grad students. They definitely looked like they were having the most fun, already hovering around the table that was set up with glasses of wine.

She fought the temptation to join them, and instead gave Marco a little wave as he caught her eye across the room. He looked right at home there, she thought, surrounded by glamorous and successful people. Probably because, outside the crazy world they'd co-habited recently, he was a glamorous and successful person himself. She knew him much better now – but part of her would always think of him as 'the other'. As the stranger she saw in the park, who seemed to be encapsulated in his own bubble of health and happiness. As the man who'd flirted with her in the shop, and left her tongue-tied and blushing. As something entirely alien to her small, quiet universe.

Maggie looked on as he made his goodbyes, and as the woman in the heels held on to his arm for as long as possible. That, she was guessing, taking in the glossy dark hair and super-slim figure, was probably the kind of woman he normally dated. What a cow.

She gave Marco a quick smile as he came towards her, using the crutches like a pro now, his leg barely slowing him down.

"You can stay if you like," she said, noting and really not appreciating the unintentionally shrill quality in her voice. "I can come back for you later – looks like you were having fun."

"Looks," he said, frowning slightly in confusion, "can be deceptive. How are you? Did Ellen get off safely?"

Maggie nodded, turning to leave the room, impossibly keen to get away from the polite chatter and the curious glances and the stink of other people's success. It was small-minded, she knew – but that was the way her day was shaping up.

"Yes, fine," she replied, pausing by the doorway and waiting for him to catch up. "How was the lecture?" she asked, realising how petty she was being. None of the way she was feeling right now – missing Ellen, sad about Christmas, and about as attractive as a goat with leprosy – was his fault. He couldn't help being what he was any more than she could help being what she was. Seeing him here, surrounded by his people, in what she knew was his natural element, had rattled her. Reality had come and given her a swift kick up the backside, and left a loser-shaped bruise on her arse.

"It was good," he said, holding on to her arm to stop her dashing away ahead of him again. "What's wrong?"

Maggie puffed out one long, frustrated breath, and tried to rearrange her face into something resembling a smile.

"Nothing. Just having a bad hair day – anyway, sir, your carriage awaits."

He followed her to the car, and Maggie waited until he had settled in before sliding the door shut. She stored the crutches in the back, and got in next to him.

"How's the leg?" she asked, trying desperately hard to find her balance. It had been a shit of a day, really. Shower-gate had left her feeling empty and unsatisfied with her lot in life in a way she'd never experienced before. Ellen had buggered off to Paris. The shop had felt cold and deserted as she worked, and she'd even found herself crying quietly as she worked on Isabel's dress, careful not to stain it as the tears fell pathetically from her eyes. But, she reminded herself again, none of that was his fault. What felt like a lifetime ago now, she'd told him off for taking out his bad temper on the male nurse who'd delivered him to her home – and now she had to try and suck down her own medicine.

"Oh, you know," he replied, dragging up the jogging pants and glaring at the cast. "Still there. Still useless. Still itchy."

Maggie looked at the cast, and the scrawled messages it had gathered during its outing at Gaynor's wedding. Smiled at the shaky writing and neon pink love hearts. And then noticed the brand new addition. Huh.

"Is that a phone number on there?" she asked, already knowing that it was. And already suspecting who had left it there. Even her handwriting was stylish.

"Uh...yeah. That woman, the facilitator? Chantal? Said she couldn't find any paper..."

Yeah, right, thought Maggie, gritting her teeth as she fiddled with the car keys. She realised her grip on them was so tight her knuckles had faded to white, and that an absolute swear bomb was building up inside her. She bit her lip so hard she tasted blood, and stared straight ahead through the windscreen, desperately trying not to let the bomb go off in front of him. She felt angry and bitter and sad all at the same time, and had an almost irresistible urge to punch something. Or someone.

"Maggie?" said Marco, taking in her stern expression, the clenched fists, the silence. "Are you okay? Are you...jealous?"

His voice rose slightly with the last word, and she noticed he was smiling. Almost, in fact, laughing. Which only made her feel more helpless. If this was jealousy, it sucked big time. She sighed, and tried to force herself to climb down from the cliff that she seemed to be tottering along. God. He was right. She was jealous. So jealous she was possibly going to turn into the Incredible Hulk, and set off all the airbags.

"Yes," she replied quietly. "Of her shoes. Now put your belt on, will you?"

He nodded, and held her gaze for a few seconds. He looked annoyingly pleased with himself, and Maggie allowed herself a brief fantasy where she delivered a karate chop to his nose. Or at the very least stamped on his big toe.

She turned the keys in the ignition, and knew she was going to have a kick-ass drive all the way home. And if anyone so much as considered cutting her up or not giving way at a roundabout, she'd be out of the car and beating them to a pulp within seconds.

Just as she was about to pull out of her parking spot, she heard the familiar ping of a text landing on her phone. Ellen, she thought, turning the engine off again. Letting her know she was still alive and had arrived. She grabbed her phone from the depths of her bag, and slid the screen on, expecting to see her daughter's familiar icon: two raised fingers, with a mass of ginger hair behind them.

Instead, she saw the message was from Isabel. She frowned as she read it, and felt the now-familiar sensation of more tears stinging the back of her eyeballs as they made a bid for freedom. She put the phone back in her bag, and leaned into the seat, screwing her eyelids closed so tight a few drops were squeezed from the sides.

"What is it?" asked Marco, reaching out to take her hand. "Is it Ellen? What's happened?"

"It's Isabel," Maggie replied, accepting his touch and the comfort it offered. "Michael's ill. He's back in hospital. And the wedding... it's going to happen there. Today."

Chapter 22

The remnants of an apparently successful Christmas party still lingered on in the Morse Bar. Named after the famous literary detective, and tucked away in one of the city's most elegant hotels, laughter and chatter echoed around the soaring arched ceilings, only falling flat when they reached the table for two in the window. The table that had no smiles, and seemed to be cocooned in its own bubble of quiet and reflection.

Maggie and Marco sat opposite each other, glasses of wine on the table in front of them, both lost in thought as they watched the new flurries of snow swirling outside on the busy street. Shoppers bustled past laden down with bags that threatened to blow out of their hands; teenagers wandered by eating chips out of open bags despite the weather, and cars edged slowly and carefully along the increasingly whitened roads.

Around them, in the cosy, wood-panelled room, were the sounds of joy and fun and the kinds of Christmas spirit that came straight from a bottle. On the table next to them, a young couple – fresh from the party and still wearing name tags – were leaning in close to each other, faces inches apart, the man resting an exploratory hand on the woman's thigh. The woman smiled, and edged even closer.

"Looks like someone's in for a good night," said Maggie, gesturing to them with a nod of her head. Marco looked on and smiled.

"Good luck to them – and at least they'll know each other's names in the morning."

She managed to find a small laugh for that one; the rarest of sounds on the hardest of days. They had come here straight from the hospital, where they'd left the newly married Isabel and Michael to start their life together in the most difficult of circumstances.

Michael had collapsed at home the day before, and after being rushed in for tests, was confronted with frowning faces and carefully phrased sentences that all added up to one unpleasant message: he was very, very sick. Nobody had spelled it out for them – they were waiting for his regular doctor to arrive – but nobody had needed to.

Suddenly, a Christmas Eve wedding had seemed too far away. A distant shore they might never reach. Michael and Isabel had asked about getting married there, in the hospital, and the staff had miraculously made it happen.

Maggie had emerged from the lift with the wedding dress, spotting Isabel and clutching her so hard she thought she'd never let her go. She'd been holding back tears, determined not to end up needing consolation herself. This was Isabel's day – no matter how screwed up a day it was. After a year of fittings, of conversations, of getting to know this wonderful young couple, it was killing Maggie that this was the way it was going to end. Not in their village church like they'd planned, but in antiseptic corridors, in a small room with a hand cleansing dispenser on the wall.

By the time Maggie and Marco had arrived, there was already a table laden with cake and champagne and boxes of confetti, as well as two perfectly dressed bridesmaids with tell-tale mascara stains beneath their eyes. Other patients on the ward had donated their get-well flowers when they heard what was happening, and Michael's room was filled with vases of multi-coloured blooms.

"Please, stay," said Isabel, when she finally pulled away. "You and Marco. We're trying to make this as happy as we possibly can – so please, share it with us. We're not giving up – we have to hope that they're wrong. For a miracle. That this is our beginning. Stay, if you can."

And so they'd stayed. Maggie had helped Emma with the dress, and the bridesmaids had taken care of the hair and make-up, filling the nurses' break room with the smell of perfume and hairspray and the delicate scent of roses that Maggie had spritzed on the inside of the dress.

When they'd finished, Isabel looked stunning. The dress was perfect – a simple, fitted sheath style, satin overlaid with embroidered ivory lace, and a matching veil. As Maggie took pictures with her phone, off-duty nurses crowded around, ooh-ing and aah-ing and admiring. The hectic preparations were a true test of waterproof cosmetics, and by the time they were all ready to emerge and meet the chaplain, not a single one of them had failed to shed a tear.

As they'd walked down the corridor – Isabel on the arm of her sombre-faced dad, bridesmaids behind, Maggie taking up the rear – patients and staff from the ward had appeared, lining the space around them, some in uniforms, some in pyjamas and robes, others in hospital gowns. They all applauded as the wedding party passed, all knowing what this meant. Knowing that a bedside ceremony had its roots in the most uncelebratory of causes. Isabel, though, didn't seem to be focused on that – instead, she walked down that corridor as though she was walking down the aisle, glowing, radiant, beautiful. Every inch the perfect bride.

One of the nurses had borrowed Marco's laptop and downloaded a version of Here Comes the Bride, and the traditional music was filling the room as she walked regally through the door, and over to the side of the man she loved.

Propped up in his bed, wearing the wedding suit that was now too big for him, sat Michael. His face was drawn and weak, and his arm was connected to a drip by his side – but the moment he saw her, the moment Isabel walked into that room, he seemed to revive. To find a hidden reserve of energy that made him shine with happiness as he reached out his hand to hers.

Maggie stayed near the back of the room, looking on as the chaplain started the service. She kept her hazy eyes on the couple, but felt Marco by her side, leaning up against the wall and putting his arm around her, pulling her in tight as the inevitable tears started to fall. She collapsed against him, glad of his strength, his comfort, his understanding. Glad to not be alone as she silently wept.

By the time they were pronounced man and wife, and Isabel leaned down so that Michael could kiss his bride, even Marco's eyes were glistening.

Against all the odds, it was completely perfect – without the church or the guests or the endless group photographs, but with everything that mattered. With love, with commitment, with joy. With absolute certainty that they were doing the right thing.

Someone threw handfuls of showering confetti, and there was the sound of a champagne cork popping. Michael's father led a round of cheers, then produced cigars they couldn't smoke. Plastic glasses were dispensed to everyone – even the patients outside in the corridor – and the fizz was poured. The party, such as it was, had begun.

When Maggie and Marco left, Isabel was still perched on the side of the bed, laughing and smiling as Michael grasped her hand with as much strength as he had. He didn't look like he ever planned to let her go.

It was, quite simply, the most beautiful wedding Maggie had ever been to – and it had left her emotionally crippled.

The two of them emerged into the carpark of the hospital to find the snow had started to come down again, whirling in wind-swept flurries as they huddled together, making their way slowly and carefully back to the car, and back to reality.

Maggie had quickly put on the heating, blowing into frost-tinged hands. The radio kicked into life – a carol service being broadcast from a local church; angelic voices bringing to life the melancholy tones of *In The Bleak Midwinter*.

She'd looked across at Marco, who was leaning back in his seat like a rag doll, the strains of the day playing so clearly across his face. He'd barely known them – but it was impossible for anyone with a heart to have survived that ceremony without taking some serious emotional damage. And Marco's heart, she knew, was bigger than most.

"I don't want to go home," she'd said simply, staring out at the snow.

"Then we don't," he replied, taking hold of her shaking hands and warming them in his own larger grip. "We go somewhere else. And we talk, or we don't talk; and we eat, or we don't eat, and we give ourselves the chance to just catch our breath. And we make a toast – to Isabel and Michael, and whatever future they have together."

That initial toast had been held over two hours ago, when the bar had been quieter, and the party presumably contained to a function room. Quietly, they'd sat there, occasionally holding hands or talking. Looking outside. Lost in their own thoughts, but together at least. There'd been wine, and food, and comfort.

Now, as the party whirled around them, and the signs of life being lived to the full arrived in the form of noisy chatter and laughter and drunken couples getting cosy in the corner, Maggie couldn't think of anything worse than going back to her empty home. Of seeing the remnants of Hurricane Ellen lying around the house. Of seeing Marco's things, and knowing that soon, they'd be gone too. Of walking past the closed curtains and darkened windows of her dad's unoccupied flat. Of confronting that bloody inflatable Santa and the drooping boughs of her own Christmas tree.

Of facing up to the fact that the life she was living was only a half life. That by being free of complications and problems and risk, she was keeping herself hidden in the shadows of what life could truly be.

She'd seen that on Isabel and Michael's faces as they exchanged rings – even there, in the hospital, they shared more joy, more vivacity, than she had ever encountered.

Perhaps, she thought, meeting Marco's hazel eyes, it was time to finally take a step forward. Take a risk. Take her chance at finding passion in her own life – even if it was just for a few days.

"I still don't want to go home," she said, leaning forward and kissing him. He immediately twined his fingers into her hair, pulling her closer and returning the kiss with the fire and energy she'd been longing for.

When the kiss ended, he held her face tenderly between his hands, and replied: "Then we don't."

Chapter 23

"This dress," said Maggie, unwrapping it from the dry cleaning plastic, "is more than earning its keep this month."

"It is a lovely dress," said Marco, from his prone position on the bed, naked apart from his boxers, muscular arms folded behind his head. "But I kind of have to say, I prefer you in what you're wearing right now."

Maggie glanced down at her matching black pants and bra, still slightly amazed that she felt comfortable walking around like this. That she'd somehow developed enough confidence to not only be naked with Marco, but to parade about in her knickers without giving it a second thought. In the space of four days, she'd turned into a shameless hussy – at least around him.

"Fair enough," she replied, abandoning the frock and walking back over to the four-poster. She climbed onto the bed, and then climbed onto the man that was lying there, leaning down to kiss him. "But I don't think it's an acceptable Christening outfit, do you?"

"The Christening," he said, clamping his arms around her waist so she couldn't escape, "isn't for hours yet. We could fit in a lot more practice between now and then. I'm getting better at this one-legged sex thing, but believe me, I can be a lot better."

She sighed as his hands slid teasingly over the curve of her back, and she felt the very male reaction she would never quite get used to. Saw the way his hazel eyes clouded with need as she wriggled against him; luxuriated in the touch of his bare chest against her skin. Trembled as his lips started to explore the sensitive hollows of her neck, flooding her entire body with a whirlpool of warmth. A lot better than this, she thought, would be completely beyond her powers of imagination.

Four days of this delectable torture, and she was still shocked by it all. Shocked by that first night together, in the hotel. Shocked by the way they'd woken up, wrapped in each other's arms, his good leg thrown possessively over her hips. Shocked by how mind-blowingly good it had been to finally give in to the feelings she'd had for this man since she first saw him – and by how good they were together.

Shocked mainly, she had to admit, by herself. By the way she had opened up, responded, blossomed under his more experienced touch. Frankly, she didn't know how it was possible – that there was any connection at all between a drunken fumble in the back of a Datsun Sunny and this glorious, aching harmony she shared with Marco. It had awoken something in her that she never wanted to lose – and so, when yet again he'd asked her to come to Scotland with him, she'd simply said yes.

Now they were here, in the hotel that the Cavelli clan seemed to have totally taken over, preparing for Luca's Christmas Eve baptism. Or, she thought, as Marco sneakily unhooked her bra, not preparing...

"We shouldn't," she whispered.

"We should," he replied, taking one of her now-exposed nipples into his mouth and rendering her incapable of further speech.

Chapter 24

The tiny chapel was crowded with Rob and Leah's friends and family. The couple themselves stood by the font, Leah keeping a tight grip on Luca's pudgy hand in case he made a break for freedom.

Marco was acting as Godfather, and a family friend called Morag – the owner of the holiday cottage where Rob and Leah had first met – was Godmother. Morag was, as Leah had described, an absolute dot of a woman.

As the words of the service were called out, and the priest reached to take Luca's hand, the kid finally managed to pull free of his mother's grasp and looked fired up to attempt a mad dash down the aisle. His little body, togged up in a suit, was pumped and ready to roll.

Rob, clearly used to the chase, pre-empted him and scooped him up into his arms, whispering a few words into his ear that made the little boy settle. He turned a surly face towards the priest, and leaned forward, looking as though he might bite him.

"I baptise you in the name of the Father," the priest said, trickling water over Luca's curly dark head, rivulets running down onto his furious face and rosy cheeks.

"Bad man!" Luca shouted, pointing at the priest. "Wet!"

"And in the name of the Son," the priest said, doing it again and provoking a scream that threatened to shatter the stained glass windows.

"And the Holy Spirit," he finished, just about managing to sprinkle the water before Luca did indeed attempt to bite him. He snatched his fingers away just in time, which led Maggie to believe that that wasn't the first time it had happened.

She held in her laughter as she watched, not daring to meet anyone else's eye in case she exploded with it. She noticed Dorothea, Rob and Marco's mother, tall and elegant with an icy white bob, also biting her own lip, eyes closed against the silent mirth that was rocking her body.

Marco gave her a wink as they trooped back to their seats at the front, scooting up the aisle on his crutches, and Leah looked like she might be about to pass out as she waddled past. This, thought Maggie, must have seemed like a great idea at the time: a beautiful Christmas Eve ceremony in the place where love had first blossomed; amid the stunning scenery of Scotland in the snow.

But just then, with a toddler showing every sign of being a natural born Satanist and baby number two itching to make its way into the world, she looked like she'd rather be in bed with a good book. Poor woman.

The ceremony drew to a close, and the guests made their way back to the nearby hotel for the reception. Some had come in cars, but others, including Maggie, were making the trek on foot, skidding and slipping up the icy country lane, wrapped in coats and scarves that were quickly blanketed in fresh snow.

By the time Maggie arrived, Leah was already sprawled on an armchair by an open log fire, a mountainous plate of sandwiches on a small table by her side, shoes kicked off and lying at right angles by her feet. Her belly was so big, encased in a red floral dress, that her arms and legs seemed to be poking out of her middle like cocktail sticks. Her blonde hair had started to escape its originally neat bun, and her hands were rhythmically stroking her own tummy as she smiled up at Maggie.

"Hey you," she said quietly. "Come sit with me. I've completely washed my hands of the demon child for a while, and as I can't even get drunk, I'm planning to just sit here and stuff my face for the next few hours. I will hate every single person here by the end of the day."

"Can't say that I blame you," replied Maggie, eyeing the drinks trays that were being offered around by tartan-wearing waiters. "How are you feeling?"

"Oh, you know," said Leah, screwing up her eyes as a pain ratcheted up her spine, "big as a whale. Stone cold sober. Sleep deprived. Nervous. But...happy. Yes. Really happy. I know it doesn't look like it now, but we weren't always this perfect little family unit. There was a lot of heartache on the way, and moments when I genuinely gave up hope on ever being happy again. I spent the whole of my pregnancy away from Rob, in London, not knowing if my baby would ever even know his own father. I felt like I'd been chopped in two pieces, and that I'd left one half of me behind in Chicago, with him.

"So whenever I feel a bit over-wrought – or over-pregnant – or when my darling son tries to mutilate God's representative on earth, I just have to remind myself of that. That I got my happy ending, and that it was all worth it. The other thing I do," she said, reaching for a sandwich, "is eat too much. The cure for all ills. Anyway – how are you? You look...different."

"I know," replied Maggie, blushing slightly at what she suspected was the other woman's totally correct intuition about why. "It must be because I'm not sitting on a rubber ring any more."

"Ha! Somehow I don't think that's it," said Leah, studying Maggie's flaming face a bit too closely. "I have the sneaking suspicion that you've fallen foul of the infamous Cavelli man charm. I blame myself of course – I should never have left you there with that evil predator..."

Maggie burst out laughing, and Leah joined in, just as the evil predator himself hopped towards them. Declaring himself completely over the shirt-and-tracksuit pants look, Marco had persuaded Maggie to cut his suit trousers off at the knee, hemming them up and leaving the cast on show. Luca had added a festive picture of a Father Christmas that consisted entirely of one red eyeball with a big grey beard.

"Hey ladies," he said, leaning down to kiss Leah on the cheek, pausing to rest his hand on her huge belly. "How's this little fella doing?"

"*She* is doing just fine, thank you," Leah replied, pulling him down to sit next to her. "I keep telling you all that it's a girl."

"I know, but I'm a man – you don't expect me to listen to you, do you?"

He glanced across at Maggie, and felt his face crease into the now-familiar smile it always seemed to wear when he saw her. When he was near her. When he thought about her. Which was, he had to admit, pretty much all of the time.

Since that first night together at the hotel, they'd barely spent a second apart. And they'd barely spent a second with clothes on, apart from while they were driving. It had been four days of absolute bliss, even with a broken leg.

She smiled back at him, but neither of them spoke. It was like this sometimes. They'd either be bantering, or silent – as though they didn't always need to talk. Just being together was enough. Marco had never experienced anything like it, and his heart cracked just a tiny bit whenever he thought about leaving her. About going back to Chicago. Going back to what was, allegedly, his real life. Saying goodbye to her pretty little house, and Oxford, and Ellen and Paddy, and mainly, of course, to her. To this quiet, warm, actually incredibly funny woman, who'd welcomed him into her life, into her home, and eventually into her bed. A bed he never wanted to climb out of.

He'd expected her to be nervous, that first night. Scared, or anxious. But he couldn't have been more wrong – she'd come alive as soon as he'd touched her. And so, he was starting to suspect, had he.

"You're being very quiet," he finally said, leaning forward so he could lay a hand on her knee, and feeling her cold fingers immediately cover it.

"I'm trying to be mysterious," she replied, gazing at him with a sparkle in those green eyes. "It suits me better. I'm not like Leah, or even Ellen – I'm not one of those women who gets noticed. I don't light up the room. I sneak in under the radar."

"Well," he said, gripping her fingers tighter, "that depends on who else is in the room with you. You light it all up for me, sweetheart...anyway. I gotta go. I've heard there's some kind of snowball warfare being planned outside, and I need to take up a strategic command position. And yes, before you say it, I'll be careful."

He leaned across to give her a quick kiss, then hoisted himself back up and towards the doorway. Maggie glanced outside, and saw a dozen or so figures, big and small, swaddled up in coats, running around on the open snow-covered garden. She watched and smiled as Marco took one step outside, and was immediately bombarded with a hail of snowballs. That, she thought, must have been his first strategic command decision. Snowball obliteration.

She turned back to Leah, who was studying her with narrowed amber eyes.

"I was right," she said triumphantly. "I didn't need to book separate rooms for you two, did I? That thing he just said, about you lighting up the room? That was one of the most romantic things I've ever heard come out of a man's mouth. Definitely from *his* mouth. So go on – tell me all. I'm practically family."

"Umm...there's not much to tell, really, Leah. It just kind of snuck up on us, I suppose. Things happened. Things changed. Things...are complicated."

"What? Why complicated? I hate that word! It looks pretty simple to me, Maggie. He's in love with you. You might as well get a T-shirt printed up that says 'The One' on it."

"Don't be silly!" squeaked Maggie, staring at Leah as though she was insane. "Of course he's not in love with me! It's just a... fling. A Christmas fling. He'll go back to his life, I'll go back to mine, and everything will be normal again."

"Right," replied Leah, frowning as she spoke. "Back to normal. And that's what you want, is it? You were happy with normal?"

Maggie ignored her and looked outside again. Saw that Marco had taken up his place sitting on a car bonnet, and was waving his crutches around like fake machine guns, as though he was fighting off a mass invasion. The invasion was coming in the form of Luca and several other children of varying sizes, all of whom were advancing on him, throwing snowballs and squealing with absolute delight every time one of them hit their target. His hat was soaked through and plastered to his head, and he looked every bit as happy as the kids.

He was so at home there, surrounded by screaming children.

Children. The one thing she couldn't give him – and the one thing he deserved.

She met Leah's eyes, and put as much feeling into her voice as she could.

"Yes," she said. "It's been fun, but that's what I want."

Leah made some kind of 'pah' noise, and put her sandwich back down on the plate. She leaned as far forward as her baby bulk would allow, pinning Maggie down with her gaze.

"I'm sorry Maggie, but I just don't believe you," she said. "I see the way you look at him. The way you look at each other. I saw it that very first day, in the hospital. Marco is a wonderful man. From when I very first met him, he's been nothing but supportive and kind. He looks like a bruiser – but he's a big softie inside. I've never understood why he's never met anyone - and believe me, there have been enough women who've tried. I suspect it's to do with Rob. With what happened after his first wife died. I think Marco started living for Rob from that point on – he put his own life on hold while Rob was having his super-long nervous breakdown, and after that – after he met me – it had become habit. You're the only woman who's ever broken that habit. Tell me you don't love him – look me in the eye and tell me that."

Maggie stared at her hands, folded on her lap. Glanced up at the roaring fire; the vast pine tree in the corner of the room, dripping with tartan ribbons. Through the window at the snowballing army. Back at her hands. Anywhere, in fact, apart from at Leah. At that pretty face, and those knowing eyes, and a woman who seemed to come equipped with emotional X-ray vision.

Eventually, when she couldn't hold in the tears any longer, when her vision became blurred with liquid heartbreak, and when the silence finally became too much to bear, she looked up. She needed, she realised, to tell someone. To talk about it. To take her finger out of the dam, after all these years.

"I do love him," she said, quietly. "I can't look you in the eye and deny that, Leah. But it can't work. Look at him out there. That's what he should have, that's what he deserves – a family like yours. You know how he is with Luca – he's a natural father. And I can't give him that. I can't have any more children. Ellen was my first and only. I...well, I won't go into the details, but I can't. And if I let this carry on, I'll be taking that chance away from him. It wouldn't be fair. I need to end it, for both our sakes. I just can't figure out how."

Leah's mouth opened and closed a few times as she processed what Maggie had just told her. Her own eyes misted over, and she reached out, taking Maggie's trembling hand in hers.

"I'm sorry," she said simply. "I'm really sorry. That is a terrible thing to happen to you, and I can understand why you feel like you do. But...Maggie, don't you think it's up to Marco to decide what he deserves? What he wants? Have you even talked to him about this?"

Maggie shook her head, screwing up her eyelids to try and stop more tears sneaking out. She probably already had mascara panda eyes, and a day-long party to get through.

"No," she replied. "I haven't talked to him about it. I haven't really talked to anyone about it. The only person who knows is my father, because he was there with me on the day it all went wrong. I've never told Ellen – I mean, that wouldn't be fair, would it? To lay that kind of guilt trip on a child. I've just...lived with it. And it's been okay."

"Until now," said Leah.

"Yes," answered Maggie, looking on as Marco crumpled up into a foetal ball on the car bonnet, over-run with yelling kids and getting completely trashed with snowballs. "Until now."

Chapter 25

Maggie let out an audible sigh of relief as she parked the car outside her house. The drive had been pure hell, especially when she was blinded by grief as she chugged along the motorway, leaning forward in her seat and blinking away tears as the spray from Polish lorries swooshed across the windshield.

She still didn't know if she'd done the right thing, and the inflatable Santa across the road wasn't sharing any words of wisdom.

Still, she thought, climbing out and stretching tired legs, she was home. After hours of overnight driving, she was finally home. Alone, but in one piece – at least physically.

She opened the front door, and kicked a few scattered envelopes out of the way as she carried her bag back in. It was almost noon. On Christmas Day. The hallway felt cold and frigid, and smelled of old pizza. She walked into the empty living room, and was confronted with Marco's bed. The sheets were still rumpled, and she knew they'd smell of him. For one confused moment, she wanted to do nothing more than climb in, and wrap herself up in the fragrance of the man she loved.

That way, she decided, lay madness. Instead, she grabbed up the sheets, pulling them off the bed viciously and rolling them into a bundle in her arms. She walked through to the kitchen, and shoved the whole lot in the washing machine. Time to wash that man right out of my hair, she thought, going into the hallway and flicking the heating back on.

They'd left the house in a hurry, and the remnants of Marco were still all around her. Two bottles of beer left on the coffee table. X Box controllers from him thrashing her at *Call of Duty* by their side. The slippers he never, ever used, claiming they were for old men and sick people, still lying on the floor. An empty blister pack of painkillers. And the Marco-shaped Action Man that Ellen had made, what felt like a lifetime ago – it had taken a swan dive from the tree, and had landed on top of the wrapped presents, toilet-papered leg sticking out at a right angle.

She picked it up, and found herself giving the plastic face a little kiss before she placed him back on the now-wilting branches.

Yes, she thought, I'm home. But everything that made it a home was missing – Ellen, Paddy, Marco. Now, it just felt like a cold, messy house, with ghosts of Christmas past lurking in all the corners.

She made herself a cup of coffee, and went upstairs. He, at least, had never been upstairs. It felt safer, calmer. Less likely to threaten the sanity she was holding on to with her fingertips. The door to Ellen's room was open, and as she walked past she saw piles of clothes, heaped on the floor, and the chewing-gummed hair straighteners abandoned on top, electric cord coiled like a snake. She quietly pulled the door to, not wanting another reminder of her missing daughter, and instead made her way to her own bedroom. To the few hours of rest and self-indulgence she'd promised herself on the way home.

She'd brought an old photo album up with her, from years back. From the days before digital photography, and the Cloud, and storing your pictures on your phone. From the days when her dad had called into the hospital shop and bought one of those disposable cameras, bringing it to maternity ward, snapping the traditional pics of exhausted mum and newborn babe.

Maggie kicked off her boots and climbed under the duvet, tugging it around her shoulders, and opened the red-bound book of memories. Flipped through the pages and flipped through the years, transported right back to that time in her life. Seeing Ellen, her tiny red face screwed up in fury, fluffy orange hair covering her head like neon duck down. Seeing herself, lying in the bed, drip attached to the stand at her side. Trying to smile, hair plastered with grease, skin drawn and pale and grey in the bright hospital lighting.

She didn't remember that picture being taken. She didn't really remember any of it. The labour had been long, and hard, and lasted for over two days. She was too young. She wasn't ready. She was terrified, and struggled with everything that was demanded of her. Her dad had tried his best, but he was still lost – still living his life in the pub, desperately lonely after the loss of his wife. All she recalled was the fact that she wanted her mum, that she even called out for her at the height of her desperation. It had dragged on so long, there were three different sets of midwives and doctors; night turned into day and day turned into night, and the staff shifts kept on changing.

When, eventually, Ellen had finally arrived, the sense of relief Maggie felt lasted only minutes. Her whole body was numb, her brain even more so, but she knew from the look on her dad's bleary-eyed face that something bad was happening. As she'd cradled her baby in her arms, wondering when the maternal joy she'd seen on TV shows would kick in, she'd become aware of a lot of activity in the room. Of a frown on the nurse's face. Of hastily called-for doctors rushing in and standing by her bed. And finally, when she looked down, of a gush of bright liquid red flowing over the sheets liked spilled wine.

They'd taken the baby from her, and pandemonium had broken out. Postpartum haemorrhage, she now knew it was called. Bleeding that just wouldn't stop. They'd tried some kind of painful massage. They'd upped the fluid in her drip. The doctor had pumped new drugs into her – all in an attempt to stop the lifeblood literally draining from her battered body.

She recalled hurried conversations, her father repeatedly asking what was happening, and the sensation of reality completely slipping away from her. She heard the baby cry, felt her dad grasping her hand, saw the doctor's lips move but didn't understand a word as he tried to explain something to her. Still staring at him with glassy eyes, she passed out.

When she woke up hours later, sore and confused, she woke up to a different life. A different future. One that involved an emergency hysterectomy and a blood transfusion. It hadn't seemed real at the time. Or even that important. The present brought plenty of challenges of its own, without worrying about the years to come. At 16, one baby was more than enough – it never occurred to her then that one day she would grieve for the babies she'd never have. That one fateful day could set her on the path she would walk for the rest of her existence – a path she would walk alone.

Maggie sipped her coffee, spilling it on the sheets and not really caring, as she flipped the album pages forward, looking at yet more photos of Ellen. As a baby, in the cot set up in her bedroom, which still had posters of the Spice Girls on the walls. She recalled how she used to play their album as she tried to get a fretful Ellen to sleep; her dad out at the pub, her boyfriend long gone. Softly singing their song, Mama, and wishing she still had her own.

Instead, she was playing at being one, and the next few years passed in a blur of fatigue and stress and the hectic brand of boredom that motherhood often entails. It wasn't until she was much older – well into her 20s – that the shock of the hysterectomy truly hit home.

On school runs, feeling like a naughty child herself, she was too shy to talk to the other mums at the gate. They always thought she was Ellen's big sister to start with, and the ensuing embarrassed silences when she explained the truth were too much to bear.

As the years passed, she saw those mums have other babies. Saw them wheeling prams down the road, saw them hoisting car seats in and out, saw their families grow and expand and their lives fill with the demands of parenting.

In that sense, Maggie's life got easier. Her dad emerged, blinking like a blind mole, from the depths of his own despair. He helped her out with childcare while she trained to be a dress maker. Lent her the money for the deposit on the house. Kept her company as much as he could. And Ellen – she just kept growing, oblivious to the chaos her arrival had caused.

From that orange-haired, red-faced baby she grew into a chubby, scowling toddler, then a gap-toothed schoolgirl. She got her own friends, her own life. Started going to town and to school discos. Changed from a child who would never sleep to a teenager who never got out of bed.

As Maggie watched all that life going on around her, she ached for more. But she ached silently, and tearily, and alone, telling herself that she was lucky to have even Ellen. Lots of women went through life without any children at all – and at least the one she had was totally perfect.

By the time she first saw Marco – the Hot Papa from the Park – Maggie was so settled in her half-life. Accepting of her losses, grateful for her gains, and with no idea what would happen to her once Ellen finally moved out, moved on, moved away.

And now, she was here. Alone, in an empty house, on Christmas Day. Looking at pictures from a lifetime ago, and wondering if she would ever stop feeling broken. If Marco was the kind of man that could ever be forgotten. If she would ever feel content again.

If, by running away in the middle of the night, fleeing into a snow-bound Scottish wilderness without so much as a goodbye, she'd done the right thing. If setting him free meant she would forever be a prisoner, trapped in her own memories.

She closed the album. Wiped the tears and the snot from her face. And went to sleep.

Chapter 26

Maggie slept restlessly, physically and emotionally drained, enduring a fractured and tormented dreamscape populated by people she hadn't seen for years – including her own mother, and Ellen's dad, who had long lived in New Zealand. Luca was there too, padding around after her in woollen booties, asking for Christmas pixies and trying to bite her fingers every time she reached out to stroke his dark curls.

When she was finally woken by the trill of her phone, she felt a sense of relief, rubbing at sore, red eyes and sitting upright as her mind was dragged back to consciousness.

The phone. The phone was ringing. She glanced at the moonlight curling around the edge of the curtains, and realised she'd been asleep for hours. That the call was probably from Ellen, or her dad. That the text messages she'd ignored from Marco needed to be deleted, that she needed to wake up. Get up. Man up. Eat, drink, and attempt to be merry – or at least not wallow in self-pity. It was Christmas, for God's sake.

She grabbed the phone, which was jittering across her bedside cabinet, and looked at the number. It was an Oxford line, and one she didn't recognise. She ignored it – if it was Sian phoning from the pub to wish her a happy Christmas, she just couldn't deal with it.

She waited until the message tone beeped, then dialled up to listen. There were five waiting for her. One started with the achingly familiar American accent she couldn't bear to hear, so she wiped it after a second. The next was from her dad, shouting his greetings, Jim joining in in the background. Sounded like the cruise was going well, she thought, with a smile.

The next was from Isabel, telling her that Michael was 'hanging in there', that they were having Christmas dinner in the hospital, and were finishing off the left-over champagne with their turkey. Maggie felt a stab of guilt as she listened to the message. She'd been so engrossed in her own pathetic misery that she hadn't even given them a second thought – to the fact that this could be their first and last Christmas together. She vowed to herself that she would call in and see them on Boxing Day, and listened to the next voicemail.

That was from Ellen, wishing her an appallingly pronounced joyeaux noel, and already sounding like she'd downed a bottle of vin rouge or two. The sound of her daughter's voice made her grin, and Maggie knew that no matter how this had all turned out, she'd done the right thing by encouraging her to go away. That this would be a Christmas to remember for her, something she'd look back on in later years, something that would forever be special. Her first Christmas away from home – and spending it with her new friends in one of the most beautiful cities on earth. That, at least, was a job well done.

Maggie pressed save on that one, so she could listen to it again later – maybe when she'd downed a bit of vin rouge herself, and had opened the gifts that were waiting for her under the tree.

There was one more message to get through, the one that had just landed. The one with the Oxford number.

"Hello," said the unfamiliar voice, "this is accident and emergency unit at Oxford General, with a message for Miss Maggie O'Donnell."

As soon as she heard the words, Maggie froze, her insides liqui-dating in fear until reality kicked in and calmed her back down. It was every mother's nightmare, getting a message that started like that – but it couldn't be Ellen. She was safe in Paris. And Paddy was safe in the Canaries. And Isabel had already called. She frowned in confusion as the female voice continued.

"We have a Mr Marco Cavelli here with us, and he's given your name and number as his emergency contact. We'll shortly be moving him to the medical assessment ward, and wanted to let you know that visiting hours are between 6 and 8..."

Chapter 27

Maggie couldn't believe she was here again. Pulling up in the same carpark, trudging through the same snow, getting into the same lift, listening to the same canned Christmas carols wafting from tinny speakers. Smelling the same mix of antiseptic and handwash and lingering illness. She might as well start bringing a sleeping bag with her, the way things were going.

First the trip here with her bruised coccyx, and Marco's broken leg. Then for Isabel and Michael's wedding. Now, for the third time in a month, Maggie was working her way through labyrinthine corridors painted varying shades of green, clutching her bag and trying to remember the yoga breathing she'd learned long ago at those distant classes with Sian.

She turned the corner into the ward and glanced around – this looked like a home for the walking wounded. Whatever had happened to him couldn't be that bad, or he'd be in intensive care. He could just have a bruised coccyx, after all. She was relieved at that, but still confused, still wary. Why was he here – in Oxford? Right now, he should be in Scotland, cursing her name and preparing to leave for Chicago. This wasn't going to plan, not at all.

She approached the nurse's station, waited quietly for someone to offer to help. Waited longer than she normally would, because suddenly, she wasn't in that much of a hurry. Was told that

Mr Cavelli was in bay 4A. She nodded her thanks, and turned away.

For a fleeting moment, panic grabbed hold of her, and she stood frozen in the middle of the corridor, an Easter Island stone head blocking the path of nurses, doctors, patients and visitors. She could just leave, she thought, as the crowds milled past her. Just turn around, get back into that lift, go back down to that carpark. She could call Leah and Rob and pass on the message that their accident-prone relative was back here in hospital, and wash her hands of the whole affair.

She could run, away from this place and away from this man and away from the emotions that were threatening to bring on a full-blown anxiety attack.

"Are you all right love?" asked an elderly man as he walked by, leaning on a stick, wearing a ratty grey dressing gown over a very surprising Take That T-shirt.

"Um...yes, yes I'm fine. Thank you," she replied, hesitantly. At least part of her hesitation was due to the shock of seeing Gary Barlow's smiling face on the chest of a disabled octogenarian. The rest was due to the fact that no, she wasn't all right at all.

"Well cheer up then. It might never happen. And happy Christmas to you."

With that, he shuffled away, leaving Maggie bewildered, bothered, and a tiny bit ashamed of herself. She took a deep breath, realised she was too hot now she was inside and under the merciless strip lighting, and slipped off her coat. She needed to get a grip, and make her feet move. One step at a time, she decided, as she followed the signs to Bay 4A.

As she reached the doorway, she looked around her. Four beds, all occupied by men. Four visitors' chairs. Four bedside cabinets. Four jugs of water and plastic glasses. Only one Marco Cavelli. Her eyes found him straight away, in the far corner near the window, his bed set to sitting position and his body covered by a puke-green blanket, the broken leg making a larger hump beneath it. He was leaning back against the pillow, face turned to the window, phone lying on his lap. Still. Silent. Asleep.

He looked completely normal – apart from the fact that his right arm was in a blindingly white cast, and draped at an angle across his torso. Jesus. A broken arm to go with the rest. Maggie felt her eyes widen when she realised what she was looking at, and she almost ran towards him.

"Oh no! Not your arm as well!" she said, rousing him from his doze and taking hold of his good hand. "What happened?"

His eyes, blurry with pain, blinked open and met her gaze. She felt his fingers wrap into hers, and saw a small smile play around his lips. Her heart spun like a Catherine Wheel and she wondered how she'd even thought it possible to forget this man – to root him out of her mind with emotional weed killer, to go back to life the way it was before they'd ever met. Maybe it would have been easier if he'd stayed away – if they had thousands of miles between them. If she couldn't reach out and touch him; smell his scent; see the way his dark hair curled around his neck. But he hadn't stayed away – he was here. Lying, yet again, in a hospital bed. With another broken bone. And somehow, still pleased to see her.

"Hey Maggie," he said quietly, stroking the palm of her hand with his thumb. "You came. I didn't know if you would. I left messages, but...well. You didn't even say goodbye. I woke up, and you were gone, and all I could do was sniff your perfume on the pillow. And then...well, all hell broke loose."

"What do you mean?" she asked, fighting off the guilt at the image of Marco, abandoned and alone. She'd done it for the right reasons, she told herself, even if it didn't feel like it to him.

"What I mean is, Leah went into labour. Three weeks early. There was complete chaos while we waited for the ambulance. Luca was

165

going apeshit until my mom corralled him with a pack of Oreos, which is probably the last thing he needed. Leah was screaming for her epidural, and Rob...well, Rob was the calm in the face of the storm, I guess. I was still looking for you, wandering around the hotel in my PJs, when it all kicked off."

"Oh no! Is she all right? Have you heard from them?"

"She's fine. I got a message a little while ago. It's a boy – healthy and loud and pissed, apparently."

"A boy," replied Maggie, unable to keep the smile from her face despite the circumstances. "She'll be gutted."

"Yeah, for about a minute or so. Anyway, before she was loaded up, she grabbed my hand, and dragged me along with her. And she told me, Maggie. Between the screams and the swear words – boy, that woman can swear – she told me. About you, about Ellen's birth. And suddenly, a lot of things fell together. A lot of things made sense. Mainly, why you'd left me. It made sense – but it still hurt."

Maggie nodded, keeping her eyes downcast. She couldn't meet his gaze, she just couldn't. She knew she'd hurt him, but she'd had her reasons – reasons he now knew. Reasons that still existed, and would never, ever go away.

"And why are you here?" she said quietly. "In hospital again. In Oxford again. How did you even get here?"

"I took a cab," he answered, as though it was the most sensible thing in the entire world.

"You got a cab? All the way from Scotland? In the middle of the night, at Christmas?"

"Yeah," he said simply. "I took a cab. Driven by Derek over there – the one with his leg in traction."

She followed his gesture to the bed opposite, where a middle-aged man with a grey-haired crew cut was reading the Mirror, apparently oblivious to the mechanism he was hooked up to. He saw her looking, and gave her a nod.

"Evening, sweetheart," he said in a heavy Scottish accent. "Crappy weather we're having, no?"

He went back to his paper and turned the page, as Maggie frowned in confusion.

"We were fine until we got to that place where Gaynor had her wedding," continued Marco. "What's it called, Fruit Tree or something?"

"Peartree," she replied automatically, pretty much able to guess the rest of the story.

"And then you had a crash?" she asked.

"Yep. Spun right out of control on black ice and into a street-light. Could've been a lot worse, I suppose, though it didn't seem like that while we were being cut out of the damn car..."

"And now you're here again," said Maggie, her tone serious and subdued. "With a broken arm to match your broken leg. I don't think I'm very good for you, Marco...every time we meet, another part of you gets shattered."

She finally looked up and met his hazel eyes. He had a whopping bruise on his cheek, which clearly wanted to be a black eye when it grew up. There were cuts and grazes across his collarbone, peeking out of his hospital gown, and his forehead was still smeared with blood where the nurses had tried to clean him up.

But worse than that, worse than the broken limbs and the blood and the scars, was the look on his face. The look that told her it wasn't only his body that was shattered – that she'd done even worse damage to a part of him that nobody could see; that by running away, she'd broken something that would never show up on an X-ray. The fact that she had matching internal injuries herself didn't seem to make her feel any better about it. What had she been thinking? She could at least have left a note, or replied to one of his many messages, or even waited until morning and left like an adult instead of a child hiding from the consequences of her actions.

She might have told herself that she was doing the right thing – that she was protecting him – but the way she'd done it had been selfish. Cowardly. And just plain mean.

"I'm sorry," she said finally. "I shouldn't have left like that. I should have stayed, and talked to you, and explained. Then you could have avoided all of...this!"

"Yeah," said Marco, holding her fingers so hard it hurt, knowing she would try and wriggle out of his grasp at any moment. Seeing the guilt and pain and confusion flowing over her lovely face. "You should have. But I know why you didn't."

When she failed to reply, and responded only with a quick, desperate breath, he continued.

"You did it because you were scared. Because what we have? What we've built over the last month? It's *big*. It's bigger than anything I've ever felt, and I'm damn sure it's bigger than anything you've ever felt. It's called *love*, Maggie. I love you, and I know you feel the same way about me. If you say you don't, you're straight out lying."

Maggie sucked in air, desperate to escape now. To get away from this hospital, with its smells and its sadness. To get away from this man, big and battered and brutally honest. Mainly, to get away from the truth – the fact that he was right. That she did love him. And that loving him, she knew, still changed nothing.

She tugged her hand away, so ferociously he almost toppled over with her, finally freeing her now-numb fingers and standing up. She grabbed her bag, her coat, prepared to leave.

"Then I won't lie to you, Marco. But I won't stay either. The reason I left – the reason this thing between us will never work – still stands. It's not going anywhere. The problems aren't going to magically disappear with one stupidly romantic gesture. Love won't heal what's been hurt. I made my peace with it all a long time ago, but I won't drag you down with me. You need to get better, and then leave. Go home. Back to Chicago, and away from me. Because like I said, I'm just not good for you."

Before he could reply, she turned, and fled, tears streaming down her face.

Chapter 28

Maggie couldn't deal with going home again. Nothing there felt safe any more. There was too much of Marco left; too many reminders of the Hot Papa from the Park. Once the bed and the chair had been packed up and sent back to the hire company, she would have to give some serious consideration to getting an exorcist in to deal with the rest of it. Maybe some holy water and Latin chants would work.

Instead of driving back to Jericho, she managed to find a service station on the outskirts of the city that was still open. A bored sales assistant barely out of adolescence was doing a brisk trade in non-festive sausage rolls for the disenfranchised Christmas losers, and she'd bought herself a steaming plastic bucket full of hot chocolate and a multi-pack of Mars Bars. It was clearly the closest she was going to get to a slap-up Chrimbo dinner this year.

She found a parking spot for the car on St Aldates, and stood for a moment in the empty street, glancing at the bright lights still on in the Christ Church windows. The building itself looked like a Christmas decoration, shining so brightly in the dense darkness of the night. The only sounds were the beeping of traffic crossings and the occasional swish of a lone car wheeling slowly through the slush.

It was, she thought, as she made her way down the footpath and to the bench at the side of the river, a very white Christmas. The snow was glistening on the rooftops of the boathouses, and the banks were mounded with it. It was only, in fact, her mood that was black.

She used the carrier bag she'd got from the service station as a make-shift seat cover, and took her place on the bench, realising that it wasn't really up to the job as soon as moisture started to seep into the bottom of her jeans. Oh well, she thought, sipping her hot chocolate and opening up a Mars Bar, what's one wet arse compared to the rest of my problems? Problems that were nowhere near so easily solved.

Marco had been right, about so many things. About why she'd run. About the way she felt. But the fact that he was right didn't mean that she was wrong – it could never work. She'd finally fallen in love, after so many years of wondering what the fuss was all about, and frankly it felt awful. Life would have been much simpler without it; without seeing the rainbow and going back to living life in shades of grey. Without realising what she was missing out on. Without understanding, for the first time ever, that being content wasn't the same as being happy.

She was a coward, she knew. She was scared – of the way he made her feel. Of the way it could turn her whole existence upside down. Mainly, if she was honest, of it being taken away from her – of a future, a few years down the line, when Marco's need for children finally overwhelmed his need for her. Of becoming dependent on that buzz, on that joy, and then losing it, being left like a drug addict without a fix. Of seeing him walk away when the paternal instincts, which he so clearly had, became too much to fight.

She had thought she was ending things for his sake – but she realised, as she sat alone in the dark, starting on her second bar of chocolate, that she was also ending them for her own sake. She couldn't take the risk, not when the outcome was so uncertain. Better to choose the time and place of her emotional death than wait for the axe to fall, as she knew it inevitably would.

She'd hit rock bottom, she realised – and now the only option was to try and claw her way back up. If she was lucky, she'd get to 'not entirely miserable' by next Christmas. Or possibly she'd just eat herself into a coma, stay on this bench, get covered in the still-falling snowflakes, and be found the next morning by a passing dog-walker. She'd be completely brittle by then, and snap in two when the police tried to move her, like a frozen ice mummy.

That, she knew, shivering in her coat, was a distinct possibility. The temperatures were definitely going sub-zero tonight. She might never see Boxing Day if she stayed here much longer. She didn't even have gloves – she'd dashed out to the hospital without them – and only the sensation of the hot chocolate through its plastic cup was keeping her fingers from frost-bite.

Eventually, she would have to go home. Start to un-Marco her house. Possibly call Nanny McPhee for an emergency de-frosting session as well. At the very least, call her dad and Ellen back, and pretend she was in Scotland drinking champagne. She wondered briefly how Leah was getting on, and felt an extra layer of sadness that a life without Marco also meant a life without Leah – a woman she had truly liked. A woman who, even in labour, had been thinking about her and Marco. She may have shared – possibly screamed – Maggie's secret, but she'd have done it for all the right reasons. Leah, after all, had found her happy ending – and she just wanted the same for them. I must at least send flowers, Maggie told herself. Maybe some alcohol.

The hot chocolate was rapidly cooling, and a third Mars Bar seemed physically impossible without some serious repercussions. It was time, she knew, to drag her very wet bottom back to the car, to fall into bed again, and to get on with the rest of her life. Tempting as it was just then, she couldn't give up. If for no other reason than if she died of hypothermia, Ellen would kill her.

She scrumpled the chocolate wrappers up into a ball and popped it into the plastic cup, sealing it all up with the lid, her fingers so numb it took her several attempts.

As she did it, she sighed, staring out at the sleek black surface of the river. It was still peaceful here, no matter how much turmoil she was feeling inside. As she mentally prepared herself to make a move back to reality, back to the car, she became aware of a new and alien sound reaching her ears.

The sound of someone swearing. Loudly. With an American accent. Of feet slipping on the snow, and a worried voice saying: "Maggie? Are you there? If not I'm probably gonna die..."

She jumped up, spilling the cup down onto the floor, and whirled around. It was him. It was really him. The crazy, insane, hobbling idiot. He was making his way along the footpath, one crutch propped under his good arm, his double plaster casts shining white in the moonlight, a bag swaying from his fingertips. With every precarious step, she imagined him falling, and rolling right into the river. She'd have to leap in after him, and Baywatch him back to the bank before they both froze solid.

"Marco! For God's sake, be careful!" she yelled, running in his direction and just about catching him as he took a tumble forward. Her arms ended up around him, his face grimacing in pain as they collided and did a half-slide, half-walk dance routine back down to the bench. She helped him lower himself on to the seat, while she stood, staring at him in disbelief. He was still wearing his hospital gown, his padded jacket on top of it – one arm in, the other hooked over his cast, the bag on his lap. His bare legs were goosebumped, his feet wearing a pair of now very soggy socks and nothing else. His poor battered face was coated

173

in a cold sweat from the effort, and she whipped off her scarf, wrapping it around his neck.

"What the hell are you doing here?" she asked, kneeling down in the snow and rubbing his legs as hard as she could, hoping to pass on what warmth she had left. She knew the emotional shock of seeing him again would catch up with her soon – but just then she was more concerned with keeping him alive.

"It seemed like a nice night for a stroll," he answered, the glib tone doing little to disguise the fact that he was freezing, in pain, and had clearly lost his grip on sanity.

She pulled a face at him, and decided to whisk off her own coat and wrap it around his lap and legs. The night air swamped her body with chill pinching fingers, and she felt her teeth start to chatter in immediate response.

"We need to get you out of here," she said. "Back to the hospital. I can't believe you did this. Will there be search parties out looking for you?"

"Nah," he said, taking hold of her hand and pulling her up to sit beside him. "I signed myself out. Against doctors' orders, but hey, what do they know? Give me a cuddle. We need to share our body heat."

She felt his good arm go around her shoulders, and she snuggled in closer to him. He was, at least on that point, right.

"How did you even get here?" she asked, feeling some of the warmth of his body seep into the side of hers, using her free hand to tuck her coat more securely around his knees.

"I took a cab. Again. Marco Cavelli, Patron Saint of Taxi Drivers. We went to your house, but it was all locked up. I tried the shop, but that was closed too. This was...the only place I could think of where you might be. The place you said you always come to think. I was pretty sure dropping the whole I love you thing made you want to think – so I followed my instincts."

"You could have tried the pub," she replied, slipping her frozen fingers beneath the padding of his jacket, feeling the faint warmth of his skin through the thin cotton of the hospital gown. "It was a close second. Look...we need to leave. I've got the car up the road there, let's get you back to hospital..."

"I'm not going until we've talked," he interrupted. "Talked properly. You can't make me move, and if you leave me, you'll be responsible for the untimely death of a man in the prime of his life. I'll stay here until I look like that snowman out of *Frozen*, and you'll have to deal with that guilt trip for the rest of your life."

"I could just leave you and call the police," she replied, feeling the world's most unlikely smile creep onto her shivering lips. It felt good to be holding him again – but it felt even better to be having a ridiculous conversation with him. "Report a pervert sighting down by the river. I'll tell them there's a flasher in a hospital gown sitting here, scaring young women who only want to be left in peace to eat their Mars Bars and feel miserable."

"Well, that's just the thing," he said, leaning his head against the top of hers, inhaling the scent of her hair. "I don't want you to be miserable. There's no need for you to be miserable. This can work, Maggie – I know it can."

She sighed, feeling the sting of tears that always seemed to hovering at the back of her eyeballs these days, as though she had some sort of lachrymose medical disorder. If they came now, they'd freeze solid on her eyelashes.

"No, Marco. It can't. We were sitting here, that time, and we discussed it then. I asked you if you wanted children, and you said yes. And you'll be a great father – I won't be the one to deny you that. No matter what you think you feel for me now, that will change. It'll fade. You'll meet someone else. Someone...whole."

"You're remembering wrong," he said calmly, reminding Maggie of the fact he argued for a living. "The words I actually used were 'maybe', and 'probably'. I never said 'yes, that's the single most important ambition in my whole life' – you're just choosing to remember it like that, because it suits this reality you've constructed in your own mind."

"What do you mean, constructed? There is only one reality. This one. The one where it's all so completely messed up that I feel like my head's going to explode."

He wrapped his hands around her face, pulling her in for a kiss that she couldn't even feel.

"You're the one who's making it so messed up, Maggie. I'm right, sweetheart. You're so scared of what's happening with us – so scared to take a chance on it – that you've built a whole world of objections around one single problem. You need to admit that to yourself. I'm not going to sit here and pretend it's not an issue – that things will be easy for us – but I'm not going to let you write yourself off like that either. Jeez, what do you think I am? Just some prize stud looking for a fertile cow to impregnate? There's more to me than that. More to us than that. I *love* you, Maggie – I love you, as you are, right here, right now. To me, you're perfect. The only thing that isn't whole is me...without you."

Maggie pondered his words, words spoken with such certainty and conviction and passion, as she wrapped herself even more tightly around him. Partly for warmth – and partly because she hoped that this belief he had, this absolute confidence, would somehow seep into her bones, like some form of magical emotional osmosis.

Before he'd arrived, she'd been thinking exactly the same thing. That she was scared. Cowardly. But that the obstacle was still real, and still not one they could easily overcome. Now, listening to him talk, hearing the complete faith he had in them, she was starting to wonder. To feel a fractional crack in the armour she'd been coating herself with. To allow herself a moment of fantasy – a moment to imagine a world where they stayed together. Where they both stayed whole.

"I saw you once before, you know," she said quietly, her lips brushing against his cheek as she spoke. "And I never told you about it."

"Yeah?" he replied, reaching down to drag her coat across both their legs. "How come?"

"Because I was embarrassed. It was in the park. I was there with Ellen. We'd been for a run, and were taking a break afterwards, sitting on a bench like this one. You were on the playground, with Luca. I was...well, let's just say that Ellen didn't stop mocking me for hours. You just looked so...full of life. Of energy. You were so good with Luca. I assumed he was your son, until a few days later, when you called into the shop. And that time I could barely speak, I was so surprised to see you. I'd been secretly calling you the Hot Papa from the Park. In my mind, that's what you were – and...and part of me thinks that's what you should still get to be, Marco. So you're right – I am scared. But I also think that kids should be part of your life, that you'll lose something so vital if they're not."

"Ah, Maggie – you need to let go of that. You need to see yourself the way I see you. Kids are great, sure – but if they're not in our future, they're not in our future. The one we can have together still shines, so bright...brighter than that fancy college over there," he said, gesturing at the majestic glow of Christ Church in the distance.

"We could look at adopting. We could set up a timeshare with Luca and Rob Jnr. We can just...be. Together. The two of us. You remember when we were talking about this? I said the most important thing was finding the right woman. And now, I know, I've found her. I'll be damned if I let you get away now, after what feels like a whole lifetime of searching – without even knowing it, I've been searching, and everyone else came up short.

"It's you, Maggie. It's you I want. Not some perfect, mythical future with another woman – a real future, with you. One that starts now. With this, our first Christmas together."

He kissed her gently on the top of her head, and extracted his arm from around his shoulders. He picked up the package on his lap, and handed it to her.

"What's this?" she said, pulling out a gift-wrapped parcel, frowning in confusion, missing the warmth of his embrace.

"What does it look like, Sherlock?"

"It looks like a present...but, how? You've been with me pretty much all the time. How did you find time to do this?"

"I used a magical new invention called the internet, Maggie. Had it delivered to Leah and Rob in Scotland – I always knew you'd eventually give in and come with me. I'm irresistible like that. Go on, open it. If you still have use of your fingers."

Maggie gazed up at him for a moment, taking in the bruises, the cuts, the stubble. The hazel eyes that were sparkling in anticipation. The way the moonlight seemed to create a halo around his face; the snowflakes that were gathering in the thick dark waves of his hair. Irresistible, she thought, fumbling with the wrapping paper.

She finally managed to tear off the sheets, and pull the gift free.

It was Alice in Wonderland. A first edition, with illustrations by Lucy Mabel Attwell. Exactly the same as the one he'd wrecked when he cycled head-first into her life all that time ago. He'd listened, and he'd remembered, and the feel of this precious item resting on her knees filled her with wonder. She'd never find another man like this, she knew – and yet here she was, blithely telling him to move on, to find someone new. To leave her behind – when that would be as impossible for him as it would be for her.

He was silent for a moment, looking at her intently, trying to gauge her reaction.

"Do you like it? If not, I can get you something else; I can—"

"It's perfect," she said quickly, interrupting him, then stopping the flow of words with a kiss. A cold, frozen kiss; one that moved more on instinct than sensation; a kiss that finally made those unshed tears flow.

When they pulled away from each other, faces still just inches apart, she said: "I didn't get you anything. I feel terrible now."

"Don't feel terrible. Just say you'll give this a chance. We've both been living for other people for too long – you with Ellen and your dad, me with Rob during the dark days. It's become a habit – and now we have the chance to break it.

"Tell me that you'll take the risk, Maggie. We can move slow, we can move fast. We can live here, we can live in Chicago. Heck, we can even get married – just don't expect me to try and get down on one knee right now. Whatever you want, Maggie. Whatever way you want to play this. I can't promise you perfection – but I can promise to love you. Exactly the way you are. Just say yes."

She carefully wrapped the book back up, protecting it from the snow. Listened to distant church bells chiming midnight. Felt her heart swell with hope and pride as she looked at the big, battered man sitting beside her, half broken and still so much stronger than her.

And she said one word.

"Yes."

Epilogue

Christmas Eve, one year later
Maggie was exhausted. She'd been to so many weddings, seen so many brides, and never quite appreciated how tiring it was, being the centre of attention for a whole day.

She was collapsed in the dressing room of the countryside manor house where the ceremony had taken place, lying horizontally on an over-stuffed sofa, staring with fatigued eyes at the tastefully decorated Christmas tree in the corner. Leah had laid a couple of wrapped gifts beneath it, and from the squishy feel of them, Maggie suspected she was about to be initiated into the Hideous Christmas Jumper Club.

Outside, a tiered terrace was draped with silver fairy lights, and beyond it snow-covered gardens stretched as far as the eye could see.

It was so pretty, she thought. Like a fairy tale. A weird fairy tale where she had somehow been cast as the unlikely princess, complete with her dress for the ball.

The dress. Even glancing down at it made her smile. For the first time, she'd designed one for herself – for her marriage to Marco.

It still seemed unreal, the whole thing. The look of total wonder on his face as she walked down the aisle. Her dad's beaming smile as he gave her away. The fact that Ellen managed to complete all of her maid of honour duties without even swearing once, at least out loud.

Unreal, and over so quickly.

She sat up, straightening the palest green taffeta, and took a few sips from the champagne glass on the table by her side. She instinctively moved to tuck loose hair behind her ears, before remembering that, for once in her life, there was no loose hair – it was all swept up into the most intricate of buns, woven into the elaborate band that was decorated with vintage pearls and crystals. She'd probably have to scalp herself to get it off, but it had been worth it.

It had all been worth it, she knew now. Every last moment of panic, every hour lying awake at night, every surge of anxiety. The last year, as Marco had predicted, had not been easy. Her cold feet were positively arctic at stages, and at least twice she'd come close to calling it off. To letting the fear and uncertainty overwhelm her.

But he hadn't let that happen. He'd stood firm, solid, and convinced – he simply wasn't going to let her go, no matter how much of a chicken she turned into. There were still things to be worked out – he'd reduced his work at Cavelli Inc, and was spending part of the year lecturing here in Oxford. She'd planned her workload so she could take the whole of summer to get to know his home in Chicago. It wasn't simple – but they were getting there.

In fact, she thought, slipping her tired feet back into her satin heels, they'd already arrived – they were married. It was official – she was now Mrs Cavelli; for richer, for poorer, in sickness and in health.

The latter had been the source of some wonderful gag material for Rob during his best man's speech – sharing the story of how they met; of the ensuing broken bones and hospital visits and exasperated agency nurses getting stuck in the middle of their growing love affair.

Nanny McPhee – here with her husband, who wasn't a toy boy after all – smiled at that one. Somehow it had seemed right to invite her – she'd played an important part in those early days, sponge bath and all.

There were guests there from Chicago, from Rob's family, from his work. Leah was smiling and harassed, Roberto Jnr – who would turn one the day after – sitting up and waving pudgy hands in his pram; Luca buzzing around the room like a hornet on speed. Definitely a day, Maggie knew, when she'd agree to that timeshare in a snap. And definitely a day, Maggie also knew, that Leah had been wishing for since she first saw her and Marco together. Leah had always had a plan – and now it had come together.

Maggie's friend Sian had come, with all three of her children, and Ellen had brought her new boyfriend, Ollie. Jacob hadn't lasted, despite taking her to Paris for Christmas. Ollie, though, he mocked her relentlessly, and never let Ellen get the last word – so Maggie thought he might be a keeper.

And right in the centre of the room, sitting together around the white-clothed tables and sparkling wine glasses, had been the Brides. The beautiful brides who had also been with them on their path to this day, who had shared their own weddings with her and Marco, and were now radiant with happiness on their behalf .

Gaynor was there, vastly pregnant and dressed in a gaudy hot pink kaftan, alongside Tony. Lucy, elegant and lovely as always, was hand in hand with Josh, looking utterly content.

And Isabel and Michael were, at least in Maggie's eyes, the absolute guests of honour. He still looked too thin – in fact they both did – but they were here. They'd got their Christmas miracle, and Michael was back in remission. Back at home. Back with his beautiful wife, and treasuring every day they spent together. It lifted Maggie's spirits almost as much as the simple gold ring on her finger.

There was a knock on the door, and before she could reply, it opened. Marco walked in, and the sight of him in his wedding clothes still made her suck in a hurried breath. He was so handsome, so happy. So completely hers – this amazing man who had worked his own miracle. The man who had convinced her, finally, that she was whole. That she was enough, just as she was.

His face creased into a grin as he saw her, sitting there alone, champagne glass in her fingers, with a slightly guilty expression at being caught in hiding.

"Tiddly again, Mrs Cavelli?" he asked, holding out a hand and helping her to her feet.

"I can't help it. My husband's a beast – it's the only solace I have," she replied, falling purposely into his arms.

"Yeah," he replied, holding her close. "I've heard that about him. And right now, he needs his wife, tiddly or not, to come and dance with him. There's a whole crowd of people out there waiting to see if we do the robot."

He felt Maggie's face grimace into his chest, and laughed at her. He knew she'd been dreading this all day. Even standing in front of their guests for the ceremony had been excruciating enough – but dancing in front of them was definitely Maggie's idea of torture.

"Come on," he said, leading her from her hiding place and out into the reception room. "It won't be that bad. And at least I have two working legs this time."

The crowd applauded as they emerged into their midst. The DJ was set up in the corner, and a disco ball was shimmering over the dimmed room. Maggie glanced around, seeing Ellen and Ollie doing tequila shots at the bar; her dad chatting up Marco's stylish mum, Isabel and Michael smiling at them in encouragement. Leah pushing the buggy with one hand, giving her a huge 'thumbs-up' sign with the other. Rob looking on with Luca perched on his shoulders.

A room full of joy, full of happiness.

Marco took her into his arms, holding her tightly, whispering into her ear as he started to sway.

"I told you this would be our song," he said, kissing her gently.

She smiled up at him, finally relaxing into arms she knew would never let her fall, as the music began.

The Power of Love.

Debbie's Top Tips for a Romantic Weekend in Oxford

A man like Marco Cavelli could probably make anywhere feel romantic – but Oxford, where his story is set, is renowned as one of the most beautiful cities in the world. Here is our unofficial guide to the most blissful spots in and around the Dreaming Spires.

Radcliffe Square:
Maggie and Marco have a fateful encounter in Radcliffe Square in the book, and it is one of the most architecturally blessed places in the city. By day, it is bustling with bikes, students, and pedestrians – but at night, it becomes quieter, subdued, beautifully lit and perfectly moody. You can feel completely cut off from modern life there, apart from the street lamps and lights from the colleges and libraries, and it's even more glorious in the snow and frost.

Magdalen College walks:
Many of the Oxford colleges are stunning, and set in pictureqsue grounds, but some of the nicest spots are to be found at Magdalen. Addison's Walk. People who have trodden the tree-lined paths before include the likes of CS Lewis and Tolkien, so you're in good company. You can stroll by the waterside, admire

the woods and wild flowers, and even see deer. What could be more romantic?

The Botanic Gardens:
The oldest botanical gardens in Britain, this place is a real oasis of calm and natural beauty in the heart of the city. There are lots of walks, quiet benches, and secluded spots to relax in – ideally with your very own Marco Cavelli! It was also visited by Lewis Carroll, and used by Philip Pullman in his Dark Materials books.

Christ Church Meadows:
Some of the scenes in the book take place down by the river, and Christ Church Meadow is a perfect place to get into the mood. Bordered by water and by magnificent Christ Church College, the setting is a mesmerising blend of natural beauty and architecture – uplifting to the senses, and wonderful whatever the season. Although the riverside gets busy, there are also lots of nearby looping walks through the woods that are more secluded and private.

The Bridge of Sighs:
Actually a part of Hertford College, this is included as much for its name as for its charms! What could me more romantic than using its nickname: 'Meet me under the Bridge of Sighs'? In reality, the bridge is in a quite busy part of Oxford, but once you had met up, you could stroll through the nearby grounds of New College, or go for a heart-to-heart in the courtyard of the Turf Tavern.

A Christmas Q&A with Author Debbie Johnson

Q: What makes a perfect Christmas?

A: For me, at this stage in my life, a perfect Christmas is all about family – seeing the excitement on my children's faces in the morning; sharing a meal with loved ones; celebrating all that is good in our lives. It's a time to count our blessings and be thankful – which is very easy to forget in the insanity that lead up to it! If the cooker broke or the dogs ate the turkey (both very feasible scenarios in my house), I'd still be happy if we were all healthy and together. In Never Kiss A Man in A Christmas Jumper, Maggie is facing up to her first Christmas alone – and although she tries to stay strong about it, that is also one of my worst nightmares. Having a young family is chaotic – but does make for the best Christmasses ever!

Q: Do you have any Christmas routines or rituals?

A: We have a few. We go and choose our Christmas tree from the same place – a garden centre in the suburbs of Liverpool – on or around December 1. I usually go into a zen-like state of trance as I wander around, looking at almost identical pine trees until one 'speaks' to me – although not literally. I'd get really worried if that happens. We also let all three of the kids choose a new decoration – which means that our tree, like Maggie's, looks like a drunken elf has vomited all over it! We've been going there since the kids were tiny, and the staff always remember us. We also go to a service at our local church called Christingle on Christmas Eve, which involves carols and sweets on sticks stuck into oranges, and that is always lovely – sometimes Christmas Eve is actually nicer, because of the sense of anticipation. It's the calm before the storm, and doesn't involve batteries, Phillips head screwdrivers or cooking!

Q: Are you a Christmas cook, or a Christmas cheat?

A: I can cook – I enjoy cooking – but I am by no means at Masterchef level. We usually go to my in-laws' house for Christmas dinner, and the two of them, despite being in their 70s, cook up an absolute snowstorm of edible goodness. My sister in law and brother in law are usually there as well, and we have an absolute blast playing party games and getting mildly tipsy.

Q: Christmas in Oxford sounds absolutely gorgeous – where did you get your inspiration from?

A: I used to live in Oxford, and despite all my travels since, I still think it's one of the most beautiful cities in the world. A lot of important life stuff happened to me there – including first love and first heartbreak, as well as first terrible hangover. One of my most memorable Christmases was spent there – I was working, at the time, as a shop assistant at Oxford Debenhams. In fact, I was working in what was known as 'decs' – Christmas decorations! We had such a laugh there, although the same playlist of Christmas songs was stuck in my head – I will forever associate

Frosty the Snowman with working at Debenhams! My mum, who has sadly died since, came down to stay with me, and I left all the Christmas dinner food in the Debenhams staff fridge, where it ended up locked in and spending Christmas alone! Despite that, it was fabulous.

Q: In the book, Maggie has a teenaged daughter – what difference do children make to Christmas?

A: Well, as any woman with kids will tell you, the difference between Christmas before you were a mum, and Christmas after is huge. Before, it's more about partying and fun and friends, and yes, family – but often squeezed in, and endured with a killer headache! After you have children, everything changes, and for a very brief spell, is dominated by them, and by creating happy memories for them. My younger children are 8 and 10 so it's still full-on – but my eldest is 18 now, and like Maggie's daughter Ellen, very much has a life of his own. I'm sure when the other two are grown up as well, everything will change yet again – I just hope they still like us enough to put in the odd appearance!

Q: What would you change about Christmas?

A: I think I'd love it if people were just a bit less stressed about it all. It's supposed to be about peace and goodwill, but sometimes it feels more like a battle! The shops and advertising are always filling our heads with what Christmas should be like – and what we need to buy to make that happen – but in reality, the things that make it special simply can't be bought. I'm as guilty of it as anybody else, and sometimes need to just calm myself down, and remind myself that being on first-name terms with the Amazon delivery driver doesn't mean Christmas is sorted!

Q: Have you ever been away for Christmas?

A: Since having children, only once – to Disneyland Paris. That was full, and one of the kids was ill, and it wasn't as blissful as I'd hoped for various reasons. It also meant leaving my mum behind, which made me realise it's just not the same without family. I've lost both my parents – in fact probably my worst Christmas was a few years ago, as my Dad's funeral was on December 21 - and that makes you value who you have left far more than staying at a nice hotel. That may all change once the children have left!

Q: Are there any particular Christmas films, music or books you like?

A: My favourite Christmas film is Bad Santa starring Billy Bob Thornton. It's a very rude, gross-out comedy with a lot of bad language in it – but it's hilarious, and ultimately, does have a very relevant theme of hope and redemption. I also have a real soft spot for Bridget Jones – book and film – at Christmas. I enjoyed writing a wedding scene in the book, where I researched popular Christmas songs – as well as the classics, the ones that resonate from my own youth are Last Christmas by Wham, and the Power of Love by Frankie Goes To Hollywood.

Q: When did you write this book – and were you feeling Christmasy at the time?

A: Writing books is odd, as you are rarely writing them at the time of year they are set! So a lot of the work on this one was done in spring and summer – I'd come home from doing the school run, boiling hot, in that very warm spell we had in June, and have to try and get myself in the mood for festive fun! Listening to the music helped; music always puts you in the right mood! My next summer book was written during autumn and winter, when it's very hard to imagine we'll ever see sunshine again!

Q: Never Kiss A Man in a Christmas Jumper features some of the same characters as your hit from last year, Cold Feet At Christmas. How was that?

A: It was wonderful! So many people contacted me after Cold Feet, asking me if there would be a follow up, and wondering what happened next for Leah and Rob, the stars of that particular story. That meant such a lot to me – that my characters had struck such a chord with my readers. You can't ask for more as an author. And as Rob just happened to have this tremendously hot, funny, caring twin brother lying around, unattached, it seemed rude not to pick up with what happened next. I genuinely felt like I was revisiting old friends when I was writing the scenes that included Rob and Leah, and hope that the readers do too – although I think anybody could read this book as a stand alone as well, you don't need to have read Cold Feet. It just helps make it more fun!

Q: Bearing that in mind, what about a follow up to Pippa's Cornish Dream?

A: Again, a few people have contacted me asking if there will be a sequel – but in the case of Pippa and Ben, I think their story is pretty much told. However, I do understand, as a reader, how much you want to stay involved in the lives of the fictional characters you love – so certainly might consider some kind of short story, maybe for free download, or as an extra in a future book, that shows them enjoying their happy ever after!

Q: So, apart from Christmas, what's next for you?

A: Isn't it funny how, once it reaches November, everyone starts to think in terms of 'After Christmas' – A.C! For me, I suspect A.C might be a very busy time of year – I have my first full-length release on HarperCollins coming out at the end of January, in both paperback and e-book. It's called The Birthday That Changed Everything, and is in fact the first book I ever wrote. It's all based around a wonderful character called Sally, and what happens when everything in her life seems to go wrong – she finds herself suddenly single, mum to two disinterested teenagers, with no real career, no real social life, and wondering what to do next. She finds some of the answers on a holiday she books to Turkey, where she meets people who change her entire life, two weeks at a time! I think a lot of women will identify with Sally, and the challenges she faces, and as most of it is set by the beach in blazing sunshine, I hope it will also cheer people up from their post-Christmas blues!

Read on for an exclusive first look at Debbie's next book,

The Birthday That Changed Everything

Available January 28th 2016

'Hits the emotion button, the story button and the funny button – all on the head. Loved it' – Sunday Times bestselling author, Milly Johnson

Chapter 1

I was online, buying myself a fortieth birthday present from my husband, when I discovered he was leaving me for a Latvian lap-dancer less than half my age.

Now, I like to think I'm an open-minded woman, but that definitely wasn't on my wish list.

One minute I was sipping coffee, listening to the radio and trying to choose between a new Dyson and a course of Botox, and the next it all came apart at the seams. The rug was tugged from beneath my feet, and I was left lying on my almost middle-aged backside, wondering where I'd gone wrong. All while I was listening to a band called The Afterbirth, in an attempt to understand my Goth daughter's tortured psyche.

The Internet wasn't helping my mood either. I knew the Dyson was the sensible choice, but the Botox ad kept springing into evil cyber-life whenever my cursor brushed against it. Maybe it was God's way of telling me I was an ugly old hag who desperately needed surgical intervention.

The fact that I was having to do it at all was depressing enough. As he'd left for work that morning, Simon had casually

Debbie Johnson

suggested I 'just stick something on the credit card'. He might as well have added 'because I really can't be arsed . . .'

He may be my husband of seventeen years, but he is a truly lazy git sometimes. We're not just talking the usual male traits – like putting empty milk cartons back in the fridge, or squashing seven metric tons of household waste into the kitchen bin to avoid emptying it – but real, hurtful laziness. Like, anniversary-forgetting, birthday-avoiding levels of hurtful.

Of course, it hadn't always been like that. Once, it had been wonderful – flawed, but wonderful. Over the last few years, though, we'd been sliding more and more out of the wonderful column, and so far into flawed that it almost qualified as 'fucked-up'.

It had happened so slowly, I'd barely noticed – a gradual widening of the cracks in the plasterwork of our marriage: different interests, different priorities. A failure on both our parts, perhaps, to see the fact that the other was changing.

With hindsight, he'd been especially switched off in recent months: spending more time at work, missing our son's sports day, and not blowing even half a gasket when Lucy dyed her blond hair a deathly shade of black. I'd put it down to the male menopause and moved on. I was far too busy pairing lost socks to give his moods too much attention anyway. Tragic but true – I'd taken things for granted as much as he had.

As I flicked between Curry's and Botox clinics, an e-mail landed. It was Simon – probably, I thought as I opened it, reminding me to iron five fresh work shirts for him. I don't know why he bothers – it's part of my *raison d'être*. If he opened that wardrobe on a Monday morning and five fresh work shirts weren't hanging there, perfectly ironed, I think we'd both spontaneously combust.

'Dear Sally,' it started, 'this is the hardest thing I've ever had to do, but I need to take a break. I have some issues I need to sort out and I can't do that at home. I won't be coming back this weekend, but I'll contact you soon so we can talk. Please don't hate me – try to understand it's not about you or anything you've done wrong, it's about me making the time to find myself. I'd really appreciate it if you could pack me a bag – you know what I'll need. And if you could explain to the children for me it would probably be for the best – you're so much better at that kind of thing. With love, Simon. PS – please don't forget to pack my work shirts.'

And at the bottom of the e-mail, rolling across the page in all its before-and-after glory, was an advert. For bloody Botox. I stared at it and gave some serious consideration to smashing the laptop to pieces with a sledgehammer.

Instead, I remained calm and in control of my senses. At least calm enough to not wreck the computer.

The only problem was what to do next. When you get news like that, especially in the deeply personal format of an e-mail, it renders you too stupefied to feel much at all. I think my brain shut down to protect itself from overload, and I did the logical thing – started making lunch. Lucy would be back from a trip to Oxford city centre soon with her friends Lucifer and Beelzebub. Well, that was my name for them. I think it was actually Tasha and Sophie, but they'd changed a lot since Reception, and I wasn't sure if they were even human any more.

They'd left earlier that morning on some sort of adventure to mark the end of the school term. They were probably sticking it to the Man by shoplifting black nail varnish from Superdrug.

My son, Ollie, was out at Warhammer club at the local library, where he took a frightening amount of pleasure in painting small figures of trolls and demons various shades of silver. He still looked like a normal fourteen-year-old, at least – apart from the iPod devices that had now permanently replaced his ears. I'd got used to raising my voice slightly when talking to him, a bit like you do with an elderly aunt at a family do, and playing ad hoc games of charades to let him know dinner was ready or it was time for school.

They'd both be coming home soon, even if Simon wasn't, and they'd be hungry, thirsty, possibly lazy, grumpy, and a variety of other dwarfs as well.

On autopilot, I opened the fridge door and pulled out some ham, mayonnaise and half a leftover chocolate log, starting to assemble a sumptuous feast. Well, maybe not that sumptuous, but pretty good for a woman who'd just been cyber-dumped.

Simon was leaving me, I thought as I chopped and spread. Leaving us. My handsome husband: orthopaedic surgeon to the stars. Or at least a few C-listers who'd knackered their knees skiing, and one overweight comedian who snapped his wrist in a celebrity break-dancing contest.

It didn't seem real. I couldn't let it be real. Our marriage had survived way too much for it to fall to pieces now. Me getting pregnant when we were both student doctors working twenty-hour days. Lucy arriving, Ollie soon after; struggling to cope on one wage as Simon carried on with his residency. The miscarriage I'd had a few years ago, which devastated us both, even though we hadn't planned any more . . . seventeen years of love and passion and anger and boredom and resentment couldn't end with an e-mail, surely?

Except I knew marriages did end, all the time. At the school where I work as a teaching assistant, the deputy head's husband had recently run off with a woman he met through an online betting website. Apparently they bonded over a game of Texas Hold 'Em and next thing she knew, he'd buggered off to Barrow-in-Furness to start a new life. And my sister-in-law Cheryl divorced my brother Davy after twenty-two years, once the kids had grown up and she realised he was only ten per cent tolerable, and ninety per cent tosser.

As you enter your forties, it feels like the bad news overtakes the good. More cheating spouses and tests on breast lumps, and a lot fewer mini-breaks to Paris. I'd seen enough marriages crumble to know the risks.

I suppose I'd always thought, maybe a bit smugly, that Simon and I were solid. Solid as a big, immovable, maybe not particularly inspiring, rock. More Scafell Pike than Kilimanjaro, but still solid.

'*Mum*,' shouted Ollie, having walked into the room without me so much as noticing his size ten feet stomping through the hallway, 'stop!'

'Stop what?' I said, wiping my hands on the tea towel. My face was wet. I hadn't even noticed I'd been crying. I wiped that with the tea towel too.

'Stop spreading mayo on that chocolate log, because it's going to taste like puke – are you going senile or what? And are you . . . crying?'

I glanced down. It looked a bit like a scene from *Close Encounters of the Third Kind*, where everybody was trying to sculpt a big hill out of mashed potato. Except ruder – because a chocolate log covered in a white creamy substance does look kind of gross.

I scraped it all into the bin and took a deep breath. The tears were still flowing. Even if my brain wasn't quite processing what was going on, my emotions had kicked in against my will. I swiped my fingers across my face to wipe the tears away, smearing my cheeks with chocolate mayo cake.

Should I tell the kids or not? Was there any point, if it wasn't real? Perhaps I needed to read that e-mail again. He had said it wasn't to do with me. That he just had some issues to work through. Maybe he'd go on a retreat to Tibet and fix himself, and all this emotion would have been for nothing.

Maybe I should wait and see what happened. What he had to say for himself. The Simon I knew, the Simon I'd loved for so long, wouldn't do this. Maybe it *was* just a rough patch. Maybe he'd come round tomorrow, see me in my finest negligee and realise the error of his ways. He'd come crying into my arms, and bury his head in my heaving bosom . . . except I don't own a negligee. Or anything more sexy than a T-shirt from the local garage that says 'Honk here for service' across the boobs.

When you've been married for seventeen years, have two teenaged children and are almost forty, you're more likely to be shopping at Mother Malone's Big Knicker Emporium than Ann Summers. Maybe that was the problem. Maybe I should have been greeting Simon at the door every night dressed in garter belts and stockings, bearing a G&T with a blow-job chaser.

'Come and sit down, Mum, I'll make you a cup of tea,' Ollie was saying, carefully taking the knife from my hands and putting it on top of the fridge. He gently placed his arm round my shoulders and guided me over to the sofa. He's already much taller than my five foot five, and it's disconcerting to have to look up at your own baby.

I realised then how seriously he was taking my newfound pallor and altered mental state – he'd actually taken his iPod earphones out, and they were dangling like silver tendrils down the front of his I Heart Tolkien T-shirt.

'What's up, Mum? You look terrible. Has there been an accident? Is it Lucy? Have you finally accepted you should have let that priest do the exorcism when you were up the duff?'

His lame attempt at humour both warmed my heart and made me feel even worse. I felt more tears welling up in my eyes, running down my face in big, fat, chocolaty drops, pooling under my chin and making my neck soggy.

I stared into space while the deluge continued, barely able to breathe between sobs, lovely Ollie patting my hand and looking slightly more hysterical with every passing moment.

He jumped up as he heard the front door slam – I don't think he'd have cared if it was a gas salesman, or a hooded figure carrying a scythe. It was the cavalry as far as he was concerned.

My own heart did an equally big jig – was it him? Was it Simon, coming home to tell me it had all been a mistake?

Telling me he was sorry? Telling me to forget all about it? I felt so impossibly weak, so impossibly broken by his proposed absence, that the thought of him walking back through that door was like being zapped by a defibrillator.

'What the fuck's going on here?' Lucy shrilled at us as she stormed into the living room. Not Simon after all. Someone much scarier.

Lucy is five foot eight, most of it legs, and does a very good storm. Hands on hips, she stared down at her weeping mother, fidgeting brother, and the tea towel smeared with the remains of mayo-on-sponge. She narrowed her eyes and threw her head back. Her hair didn't budge – probably because it was dyed midnight blue-black, straightened, and glued to her head with industrial-strength hairspray.

'Tash, Soph!' she yelled. 'Bugger off, will you? Mommy dearest is having some kind of spaz attack and I need to deal with the dramatics . . .'

I heard a very impolite sniggering from the hallway, and a slight creak of the door as the Devil's Daughters sneaked a peek at the crazy woman.

They might listen to a lot of songs about the unbearable agonies of stubbing your toe on a guitar amp, but they had no empathy with a real-life human being at all. They'd be more upset at missing an episode of *The Vampire Diaries* than seeing me in tears, and I'd known them since they were four. They departed in a fit of giggles.

Lucy looked down at me, not knowing quite how to behave for a change. Her usual loving approach – verbal abuse combined with facial representations of complete contempt

– normally served her well, but she was clearly a bit unsettled by all the tears.

'Okay, Mother, what's the big deal? I know this is probably just some stupid retarded midlife crisis, but I'll give you the benefit of the doubt – have you got cancer?'

Momentarily thrown by a worldview where having cancer was preferable to a midlife crisis, I managed to stop my sniffling and stem the torrential waterworks. Attagirl, Lucy.

'No, I haven't got cancer,' I said, feeling poor Ollie deflate slightly beside me with relief – he'd obviously feared something similar. But, unlike my darling daughter, he'd actually given a shit.

'It's your dad . . .'

'Has he got cancer?' interrupted Lucy, kicking her Converse-clad feet impatiently against the coffee table. She was dressed in leggings with black and purple hoops, and could have passed for the Wicked Witch of the West.

'And if he has got cancer, is it in some disgusting place like his testicles? Because I'm telling you now there is no way I am going to sit around listening to people discuss my dad's balls—'

'No, no, your dad's balls are fine . . . well, I suppose they are, I haven't seen them up close recently . . .'

'Oh, gross, Mum!' cried Ollie, making gagging gestures with his fingers in his throat and pretending to vomit. Lucy looked similarly disgusted at the mere mention of me in close proximity to her father's genitals. Clearly she preferred the theory that she had been hand-delivered by Satan's stork.

'Oh, just shut up, both of you!' I said. 'Your dad, and his testicles, are okay – but he's leaving us. No, that's not right.

Not us – me. He's leaving me. For a while. Just for a bit, while he gets his head together. I'm probably being dramatic for no reason. But . . . well, I only just found out. He told me today. Kind of. He e-mailed me today, actually—'

'Hang on a minute – did you say e-mail? Are you telling me he frigging *e-mailed* you to say he was doing a runner?' asked Lucy, incredulously.

'Yes, well, you know how busy he gets at work . . .'

'Oh for fuck's sake, Mum, *you*,' she replied, leaning down over the sofa and poking one of her fingers in my face so hard that I went cross-eyed, 'are such a loser! He *e-mails* you to say he's walking out and you justify it because he's busy? This isn't about him, it's about you. You're a doormat. You've got no backbone. You're just a human being made of fucking jelly. No wonder he left you – you probably bored him to death!'

Exit Lucy, stage left, in a cloud of sulphurous smoke. I could practically feel the ceiling shake as she stomped up the stairs to her room, slammed the door, and started blasting music so loudly through her speakers that nomadic tribespeople in Uzbekistan would be wondering where the party was and if they should bring a bottle.

Oh good. The Afterbirth again. My favourites.

Chapter 2

'Nobody else my arse,' said my sister-in-law Diane on the phone from Liverpool. 'There always is, Sal. It's rule number one in the big book of rules about men – they never, ever leave a woman unless there's someone else to go to, no matter how miserable they are. They treat their sex lives like a relay race – they always need to pass the baton . . .'

Phallic imagery aside, I knew she had a point. And Di should know. She was married to my brother Mark, who was pretty much the best of a bad bunch, but they'd really gone through the mill when they were younger. He'd had affairs. She'd had affairs. It got to the stage where they needed a PA to remind them of who was shagging who. Eventually all the mistresses and toy boys became a burden, and they decided to have an affair with each other instead. Two decades on, they're still married, so they must have done something right.

It was the day after my exciting e-mail treat, and the kids were handling it about as well as could be expected. Lucy was out, probably scaring toddlers in the local park as she sat having a fag in the playground with the Demon Twins. Ollie was upstairs in his room, playing Lords of Legend online.

And Simon was due to come round any minute.

'But he says he needs to find himself, Di. Don't you think there could be some truth in that? We've all been so busy for so long since the kids came along, and there's his work. What if he genuinely just needs a bit of time and space?'

'Yeah, right,' she snorted, 'of course. Let's face it, Sal, any man who spends as much time in front of the mirror as Simon does shouldn't have any problem with finding himself. And, as for his work, are we supposed to feel sorry for him because he's successful? That could've been you if things had worked out differently. I know you wouldn't be without the kids – well, not Ollie anyway – but if Mr Lover Lover Man hadn't got you knocked up when you were still a student, you'd be a doctor too.

'He couldn't have done everything he has without you at home backing him up. So don't give me that "finding myself" crap. Take my word for it, he's got some little tart he's shacking up with who gives him seven blow jobs a day and treats him like God. I know it's not really in your nature, but you need to find your inner bitch. He deserves it for dumping you by e-mail.'

'I know,' I said, 'I keep thinking I might have missed something and opening it again . . . For a while I convinced myself it wasn't real, it was some kind of freaky spam . . . Anyway, better go – he'll be here soon. Thanks for all the advice and I'll try to stay tough, okay?'

'Okay, love, you do that – and you better not have ironed those bloody shirts!'

I put the phone down, still marvelling at the thought of a woman who had the time – never mind the oral dexterity

– to give seven blow jobs a day. How would that even be possible? She'd have to go to work with him, and live under his desk. And it could be really distracting when he was in surgery – she'd have to scrub in, and even then I'm not sure it would be hygienic . . .

Had Simon and I ever reached those levels of sexual athleticism? Maybe – but if we had, we'd been too drunk to notice. I was only twenty-one when we met, and sex at that age is all about enthusiasm, not expertise. And, in our case, it was also all about the contraception. Or lack thereof. Before long I was puking my guts up on morning rounds at St Sam's, realising I was pregnant with the blob of cells that would become Lucy. She was a lot less trouble then.

I spent the next four weeks vomiting. Simon spent the next four weeks planning our wedding – or at least his mother did, as soon as she found out what was going on. She was a force to be reckoned with and we weren't left much choice. Within minutes of peeing on the pregnancy test, she told us when and where we'd be getting married. I was too tired to care really, and Simon – well, he'd come from money, and respectability, and having a bastard child in his twenties was never going to be part of the plan.

Up until now I thought we'd made the right choices. For everything I'd given up, I'd gained tenfold. A good man, two healthy children, a nice home. It was more than most people got, and I'd been content. On the whole.

But maybe I'd got it all wrong. Maybe I should have spent more time getting blow-job lessons at the local College of Sex. Seven times a day? Really, was it possible?

Simon had texted me to say he'd be round at eleven, so he must be taking a break from his BJ schedule for at least an hour. He was always on time for everything; it was a point of pride with him, so I had exactly ten minutes left. Ten minutes left to rehearse speeches I knew wouldn't come out right, as I didn't have a clue how his side of the script went. I didn't know if Diane was right about there being someone else, or how I'd cope with it if there was.

I'd got up early, exhausted after a disjointed and dream-ridden night's semi-sleep. My eyes were swollen and stinging from fatigue and tears. I'd walked the dog, cried, had a shower, cried, done the ironing, cried, and had a Force Ten row with Lucy, all before calling Diane. I'd also tried on three different outfits and rearranged my hair several times before giving up in disgust. I mean, where are the style guides on How To Look Good Dumped? Or What Not To Wear While Confronting Your Probably Cheating Husband? You never see that on bloody telly, and I bet it's not just me who needs it.

Physically, I'm not in bad nick considering I am, as my kids charmingly put it, 'halfway to dead', but I'm definitely at the stage in life where the perfection of youth is a distant memory.

I'm in a gym, but in all honesty the only pounds I lose are from my bank balance. I had been hopeful that the sheer effort of carrying round a membership card in my purse would reinstate me to my size ten glory days, but apparently not. What a con.

I still fit into a size fourteen, or at least most of me does. But I have a wobbly blancmange tummy that never left after childbirth, and my derrière is, diplomatically speaking, comfortable. My boobs are too big for their own good, and need an awful lot of help from a very strong push-up bra fairy. I'd 'let myself go', as my gran might have said.

Eventually, after a load of fretting that did nothing but get me hot and bothered, my hair had ended up in its usual slightly unruly shoulder-length bob, and I stuck with jeans and a T-shirt. I had no idea what to go for – seductive, dignified, aloof? All I felt was shattered and confused. And I knew the fact that I was focusing so hard on clothes and preparations was just a way of avoiding the ugly truth: the fact that my marriage, and life as I knew it, could be over.

I heard the key in the door, accompanied by an inappropriately cheery 'Hello!' as Simon arrived and let himself in.

He was wearing a pair of new jeans – at least jeans I'd never seen before. Skin-tight on the thighs and boot cut. His fair hair was styled slightly differently, swept straight back and gelled rather than parted in his traditional 'trust me I'm a doctor' look. And he smelled – a lot. Of some quite powerful cologne or aftershave that he'd never used around the house. He looked younger, and cooler, and actually pretty damn handsome. It was him – but not him. It was his sexier evil twin.

'You're having an affair with some little tart who gives you seven blow jobs a day and treats you like God, aren't you?' I said immediately.

I just knew – from the second he walked into the room, I could tell. It wasn't only the new style and the new smell – it was the new swagger.

He was trying desperately to hold a serious and sympathetic expression on his face, but I could see it there in his eyes: a newfound confidence, self-belief . . . happiness, I suppose. The bastard.

He sat down next to me on the sofa, taking my hand in his and looking at me with that same sympathy. The look I'd seen on his professional face so many times over the years. The one that said: 'I am the bearer of bad news, but don't worry, I'm here for you.'

'Don't lie, Simon – I can see it all over you. There's somebody else, so don't deny it. How long has it been going on?'

'Oh, Sal,' he said, 'I'm so sorry . . . I never wanted to hurt you, I really didn't . . . I wasn't looking for this. It just happened. We've drifted apart so much in recent years. I honestly don't think you're happy either . . .'

I slapped his hand away and looked straight ahead. I couldn't bear to see that sparkle he was trying to hide, the way he was sad about destroying me, but unbearably happy for himself. The emotional conundrum of the newly freed male.

'What do you mean you weren't looking for it? Did you accidentally fall into another woman's vagina, then?'

'There's no need to be crude about it, Sal; it's not like that! It's not just the sex . . .' – the never-ending, headboard-pounding, scream-out-loud sex, I added in my own mind's eye – 'it's more than that. I'm in love with her. You have to believe me when I say I'd never do anything to intentionally make you suffer, or the kids. I wouldn't be doing this if it weren't serious. But I just couldn't go on like we were any more. You must know what I mean!'

Uhm ... no, actually. I'd been perfectly happy the way things were. Or, at least, definitely not unhappy. I obviously had a much higher boredom threshold than he did, and significantly lower expectations of how exciting family life in the suburbs was supposed to be. Simon, though, seemed to mean what he was saying, and appeared confused that I didn't 'get it' – he genuinely thought we'd both been unhappy, that this was somehow inevitable or necessary, a natural progression rather than a thunderbolt from the blue.

'So who's the lucky woman then?' I asked, focusing on the mistress straight away. The other issues – the fact that he'd seen our marriage in a totally different way to me – were too complicated to tackle just then. The fact that he was shagging someone else was, in a twisted way, more palatable.

Even as I spoke, I recognised that my tone of voice could curdle milk. I sounded like a bitter old hag, and might as well buy seven cats and stop washing right now.

'Her name is Monika,' he replied, intonating the name with such reverence that he could have been talking about the Virgin Mary. Except not in this case, it would seem, unless the Blessed Mother had taken a very unexpected turning in life. 'We met in a ... in a hospitality venue I visited when I was on that Ortho conference in London in March.'

'The one you said was full of cranky old men talking about hip replacements over their peppered steak? And what's a "hospitality venue" anyway? Is it double-speak for a pub or a ...'

The light slowly dawned as he started to shuffle slightly nervously next to me, casting his eyes down for the first time.

'A strip club? A strip club. You're running off with a fucking stripper. My God, Simon – could you *be* any more predictable? You're giving up your wife, your home, your kids and your bloody dog, all for the sake of someone who shakes her tits for a living?'

His head snapped up again, and I could see I'd hit a nerve. 'She's not just some slapper, you know! Back in Latvia she was training at catering school, then the opportunity came up to travel to London. She's a really intelligent girl, I'm sure she'll do very well for herself once she goes back to college!'

'In Latvia? Back to college? Please tell me you mean as a mature student . . . how old is she?'

A beat of silence. He didn't want to tell me. This was going to be bad – very bad.

'HOW OLD IS SHE?' I yelled in his face.

'Nineteen,' he mumbled, jerking his head back in shock, 'she's nineteen, all right? But that means nothing. Where she's come from, that's mature. She's been through more than most people have already. It's not easy growing up in Latvia, you know. There wasn't much money, no jobs, no way out. She needed—'

'She needed a really stupid man, Simon, that's what she needed. A really stupid man with a bit of money and his brains in his balls. And it looks like she got exactly that. It's pathetic . . . Ollie and Lucy are losing their father because you can't keep it in your pants? Have you any idea how much this is going to hurt them?'

'But it won't,' he replied, edging away from my anger. 'They'll understand, even if you don't. They're older now

– we've done a good job raising them. They've had a solid start in life, and they don't need us to be together for their sakes any more. They'll know I deserve a chance to be happy and in love – and so do you. And there's no problem with the house – obviously you'll keep that for as long as you all need it – or with money. I'll make sure you're all provided for . . .'

I was momentarily struck dumb by his use of the phrase 'together for their sakes'. Was that how he'd been feeling? Is that what our marriage had been? Had I been so stupid I hadn't noticed – or was Simon rewriting our history to justify current actions he must be ashamed of, deep down?

It was as though I was talking to a stranger – and one who certainly didn't understand at least one of his children.

'If you think for a minute that Lucy is going to accept this in any way,' I said, 'you're even dumber than you look in those sprayed-on jeans. She'll hate you for it. And I don't blame her.'

I don't know how he'd expected this conversation to go, but I was clearly not reacting the way he'd expected. He looked almost afraid as my voice rose. He stood up, retreating by several steps and taking refuge by the bay window – presumably so he'd have witnesses if I whacked him round the head with a paperweight.

'Don't worry, Simon, you're not worth it. If I'm not what you want any more, that's your choice. Before you came here today I was really hoping we could patch things up. That we could put things right – that I could try and be more like you want me to be. But without the aid of a time machine, that's obviously not going to happen. I can't believe you're leaving me for someone who's not much older than your own daughter. We've gone through all these years together and you throw it away like it means nothing . . .'

My quieter tone calmed him, and he took a step forward, holding out his hands in supplication. How could somebody so familiar, so beloved, suddenly be a complete alien? I suppose we'd taken each other so much for granted over the years that it seemed unbelievable that anything could change. Now here he was in front of me, as a totally different person. Amazing what the love of a bad woman can do for a man.

I wanted to kill him, and spit on his bleeding corpse. And I wanted him to take me in his arms and tell me he'd stay, that everything was going to be all right. I wanted the whole damn mess to just go away. I wanted my husband back. I wanted to sleep for ever. The shock of it all was starting to really kick in, and I didn't know where to put myself. The anger of my words was real – but the changing landscape of my future life was now becoming a hideous reality, a poisonous shift that I could do nothing to control or avoid.

'I'm sorry, Sal,' he said, sounding genuinely regretful. 'If there was anything I could do to make you feel better, I would . . . but I belong with Monika now. If I don't try and make a go of this, I'll never forgive myself – and I won't be much use here with you, either.'

I gulped back the sobs I could feel coming. I needed to weep and wail and beg God to help me, but that was between me and the Almighty. I'd never forgive myself if I broke down in front of Simon.

'You'd better go then,' I said, waving him towards the door. 'Leave the keys behind. Call to arrange a time to see the kids.

Your bag's in the hall. And yes, I did pack your five freshly ironed work shirts.'

With five freshly burned holes through the backs, I silently added. But he didn't need to discover that until Monday morning, did he?